Trish would ~~tell~~ W9-CHU-774
their bab~~y~~

He'd be stunned at first, then his face would break into a grin of pride and he'd hold her tightly—no, carefully—and—

Still dreamily thinking of the wonderful moment when Adam would know he was going to be a father, she noticed a fax message chattering its way out of his computer. Curious, she bent to read it. And she froze in horror....

She's sexy,
successful...
and
PREGNANT!

Relax and enjoy our new series of stories about spirited women and gorgeous men, whose passion results in pregnancies...sometimes unexpected! Of course, the birth of a baby is always a joyful event, and we can guarantee that our characters will become besotted moms and dads—but what happened in those nine months before?

Share the surprises, emotions, dramas and suspense as our parents-to-be come to terms with the prospect of bringing a new little life into the world.... All will discover that the business of making babies brings with it the most special love of all....

EXPECTING! continues next month with
Dante's Twins by Catherine Spencer
Harlequin Presents® #2016

SARA WOOD

Expectant Mistress

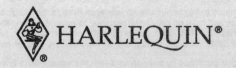

TORONTO • NEW YORK • LONDON
AMSTERDAM • PARIS • SYDNEY • HAMBURG
STOCKHOLM • ATHENS • TOKYO • MILAN • MADRID
PRAGUE • WARSAW • BUDAPEST • AUCKLAND

ISBN 0-373-12010-9

EXPECTANT MISTRESS

First North American Publication 1999.

CHAPTER ONE

ADAM was shockingly late for his own engagement party. But worse than that was the reason for his lateness. He was thinking of another woman.

In the middle of dressing, checking the fax and answering the ever-ringing phone, he'd knocked a photograph from his desk. It was in his hand and he was staring at it. His late wife. Stepdaughter Petra...and Trish.

Slowly his tense, irritated expression evaporated. Their last moment together was one he'd never forget. His hand shook a little. The photo was replaced. Heavy gold cufflinks inserted. Then he was still.

The phone and the fax demanded his attention but he was oblivious to them. In the middle of the room, he stood staring into space—and the past.

He saw her turning to him, her face beautiful in its compassion, her lips treacherously parting over pure white teeth. A feeling of profound emotion had swept over him, and an awe that he should know such a woman, speak to her, be near her...

He had no idea what had happened, only that her soft cheek lay against his, the perfume of her hair overwhelming him till he had to bury his face in it, kiss her warm scalp and nuzzle his way down to the long, pure column of her neck. And, once he'd touched her, he'd been unable to hold back.

He could feel the peachy texture of her skin even now. The pliancy of her young and supple body. Breasts high and generous, pressing against his chest. The way she'd responded like an innocent, with the unleashed passion of a gypsy.

And then he'd come to his senses.

Suddenly his usual dynamic self again, he dealt rapidly

5

with two calls then scanned the faxes and made notes in the margins for his secretary. He strode like a whirlwind through the foyer of the exclusive apartment building, and no one would have guessed from his decisive, assertive manner that he could still feel Trish's body, warm and yielding against his hands.

In a specially reserved suite in a London hotel, Trish was getting ready for the party. The invitation had been stuffed in her bag, out of sight.

Adam and Louise.

Four outfits were strewn on the bed and her damp palms bore witness to her nerves. How did you greet a man who'd kissed you suddenly, without warning, fiercely claiming possession, his kisses bruising and burning and shocking you with their passion?

Weak at the knees, she sank to the bed. She could see him when she closed her eyes. Feel his harsh breath heating her throat, and his mouth, his teeth and his tongue savaging every sensual inch.

She lay back, her arms stretched above her head in glorious remembrance. There had been no preliminaries. No courtship. They hadn't held hands, exchanged a goodnight kiss or progressed to cuddling on a second date. There hadn't been any dates. It didn't matter. That coming together had been instant, primal and inescapable.

Her heart lurched with a sweet, hurting affection as she recalled how frantic and fumbling his normally capable and careful hands had been as they'd attempted to unpick the buttons of her shirt. He'd wanted her to distraction. She'd felt giddy with power, thrilled to be the kind of woman who could create such havoc.

Her whole body had been screaming for him, every part of her hot and molten and dominating her mind, a mind hopelessly incapable of any sane thought. Her eyes had pleaded with him to tear the clothes from her body and his so that she could feel his skin against hers, gently fasten her teeth on him, taste him, know what it was like to smell

and lick that male flesh, to be totally and utterly abandoned
for the first time in her life.

'Trish,' he'd groaned, barely audible.

She'd known then that something was wrong. He had
tensed throughout his body, every inch of him suddenly
rigid. Pain had slashed silver paths across his dark eyes.
Her hands had clutched at him...and he'd pushed her away.
Before she'd even been able to speak, croak, plead, he'd
been stumbling from the room.

'You look very nice.'

Trish sat up guiltily as her friend appeared suddenly in
the hotel room and shattered all her sinful memories. 'You
might have knocked!' she complained, coming out of her
reverie with reluctance.

'I did, duckie.'

Trish frowned. 'I didn't hear a thing!'

'You were miles away,' Petra said. 'And you ought to
lock your door.'

'I keep forgetting,' Trish admitted. 'I'm not used to locking up. We never do, at home. Now you're here, help me!
Do I wear this, or my jeans, or fling myself down the lift
shaft?' she asked earnestly, turning to more immediate dramas.

Petra put an arm around her friend. 'Wear what you've
got on. Honest, Trish, you *do* look nice.'

Nice. What kind of compliment was that? Unfortunately,
the mirror told her what Petra must be seeing: a decent,
dull, unsophisticated woman. Someone who'd have difficulty even exciting a lecher who'd been marooned alone
on a desert island for ten years! She felt a surge of intense
anger.

'I don't want *nice*! I want sensational!' Trish stopped
scowling at her offensively *nice* and deeply boring dress
and eyed Petra balefully instead.

'Oh, yeah? Why? Thought you never cared about your
appearance?' Petra asked, with a sly grin.

Did Petra know her guilty secret? Trish picked up a pair
of nail scissors and tried to even up her zigzag fringe while

she dealt with her fears. Then she came to her senses. Petra would never have invited her to her stepfather's engagement party if she did.

'I'm having the jitters at the thought of all the stunning women at this party!' Trish replied, since that was half the truth. Muttering crossly, she put down the scissors in defeat. 'Women without jagged holes in their fringes!'

'And one woman in particular.' Her friend put her head on one side and critically surveyed Trish's pitch-dark hair, which had been cut by her grandmother into something only vaguely resembling a bob. 'Adam's fiancée is perfection itself,' she offered irritatingly.

Trish resisted the temptation to stamp her foot like a petulant child and wondered instead why she felt so bad-tempered all of a sudden. It dawned on her that she'd hoped Louise would be all teeth, acne and glasses! She laughed at her idiocy. Of course Adam would marry someone stunning.

'Exactly!' Experimentally, she puffed out her chest and sucked in her stomach. She just looked stupid so she let it all go again. 'Look at me! I need loads of praise, if you please. What's the use of having a best friend if she's not going to lie through her teeth and swear I'm knockout gorgeous?' she demanded with a grin.

'OK.' Petra assumed the air of a pop fan who had just seen her idol walk in. 'Wow!' she gushed, clasping her hands in wonder. 'I really, really wanna dress like that too! You'll *slay* Adam! He'll call his engagement off pronto!'

'If you're that thrilled with the sight of searing emerald polyester, I'll send you the catalogue it came from!' muttered Trish, turning away from the sight of herself in the full-length mirror. Suddenly this wasn't funny at all.

Here she was in a mail-order frock, hedge-backwards hairstyle and borrowed stilt-walker shoes—why did Petra's feet have to be a size smaller than hers?—feeling hugely inadequate, nervous, about to meet Petra's unfairly young stepfather for the first time since...

Trish blanked out the past and haphazardly stuffed things

into her handbag. Which didn't match her dress or the wretchedly crippling shoes. Everything was wrong! Feeling a total mess, she sank dispiritedly onto the bed.

Petra accurately read her friend's body language. 'If you want sensational, we could sneak off to Adam's flat, pinch a pair of his shocking pink boxer shorts and twist two silk hankies into the shape of a bra for you to wear,' she suggested helpfully.

The thought of wearing Adam's boxer shorts made Trish feel quite peculiar. 'Adam isn't the pink sort,' she said flatly.

'Purple-spotted? Fluorescent?' goaded Petra, going too far as usual.

'No!' Trish saw Petra's eyebrows rocket skywards. 'I mean I don't know what he wears beneath his pinstripes!' she cried. And never would! She put on a prim look. 'Anyway, where's your respect for your stepfather?' she asked grumpily.

'Well...' Petra was idly trying Trish's Pale Sunrise lipstick over her own gaudy gash of scarlet. 'Granted he's been my dad since I was a three-year-old brat, but he's sort of grown younger while I've grown older. I see him as being more my age. And yours.' Her eyes slanted to Trish's, gauging her reaction. 'Adam's not exactly an old wrinkly, is he? Bags of energy, lean and toned as a teenager, thanks to his personal trainer,' she said complacently.

'Sounds like you're trying to sell him on a slave market,' Trish said wryly. As if she didn't *know* he was a hunk!

'Well, he'd get a rattling good price,' said the irrepressible Petra. 'Active mind, active body. My girlfriends always get jelly-leg syndrome when they see him.'

Trish grinned. She knew the feeling. 'Sugar-daddy syndrome, you mean.'

But the image of Adam's fierce vigour made a mockery of her attempt to think of him as approaching middle age. Despite his Jermyn Street handmade suits and well-groomed appearance, he'd always projected a dangerous, tough-guy look. Perhaps, she mused, because he enjoyed hair-raising pursuits. Speedboat racing. Off-piste skiing. Risky investments. Sugar-daddy didn't come anywhere near it. Robber baron more like.

Tall. Jet-black hair...tousled by her hands... She jammed her teeth together, determined not to start that again. But he stayed in her mind, his near-Roman nose and dark good looks conjuring up an air of menace. This was more than reinforced by the unnerving breadth of his shoulders and the sublime air of authority which swept him through a restaurant to the best table in a matter of seconds.

Her eyes softened to a warm misty blue. His hard, angular jawline had felt as smooth as a baby's when she'd touched it. Dreamily she recalled the way his mouth didn't entirely fit his hard, macho look, because it was too soft and curved for ready laughter. Or kissing. And that devastating combination of total masculinity and sensual promise had been her downfall.

Trish drew in a quick, sharp breath, physically disturbed by her thoughts. Drat him! Would he never go away?

'Dear old Adam! It's nice he's found someone, at his age,' she said patronisingly, trying hard to convince herself of that fact.

Petra looked at her curiously. 'His age? Are you mad? Adam married Mother when he was eighteen. She was ten years older. He's only fifteen years older than I am. Sixteen more'n you.'

'Wow! *That* old!' Trish exclaimed in assumed horror.

Thirty-eight, to her twenty-two. In his prime.

Trish began emptying her handbag for no reason at all other than aimless occupation. He was too old—and yet too young. She thought crossly that if Adam had been the same age as Petra's late mother, or even years older, she wouldn't be in this stupid state of nervous anticipation and semi-hysteria. It wouldn't matter a damn what she looked like. Because they would never have nearly...nearly...

'What are you doing?' asked Petra mildly.

'I'm...I'm removing biscuit crumbs from the bottom of

my bag,' she jerked out, hoping her friend wouldn't notice she was having trouble with her breathing.

'Uh-uh.'

That was the most significant-sounding 'uh-uh' that Trish had ever heard. But what was the big deal about a tidy handbag? Her gaze fell on the invitation. She folded it in half and jammed it into her purse, then resorted to a search for inner calm while she studied her appearance critically.

'Petra...tell me something. Have I become a total peasant from living like a swineherd?' she asked, trying to make that sound more like a joke than a desperate bid for reassurance. Her sea-blue gaze lifted to Petra's amused and affectionate face.

Petra looked wonderful. Expertly made-up and flawless. The natural look had been perfected. Trish had tried some of Petra's foundation but she'd felt strange with it on her skin so she'd washed it off. Her brows and lashes were dark enough not to need mascara and her lips and cheeks had their own rosy tint, but she did feel that she lacked glamour without artificial aids.

In the elegant surroundings of her hotel room she looked totally out of place. No wonder people had stared at her as she'd crossed London and headed for South Kensington! They must have thought she'd fallen from a tractor and lost her way! She vowed to buy moisturiser and slap it on every night.

'I look terrible, don't I?' she said in despair.

'Stop fishing for compliments! You're so lovely, I'm tempted to stick a paper bag over your head. You positively glow with inner health, have a fab tan and legs up to your armpits. You're a breath of fresh air, you vile woman,' said Petra warmly, hugging her. 'Every artificially enhanced female at the party will queue up to scratch your eyes out.'

Trish wasn't flattered to be called a breath of fresh air. Right now, she'd swap the goose-girl look for a classy outfit, an alabaster skin, false eyelashes and long nails. She tucked her work-worn hands beneath her bottom. Too much washing up, hauling boats up slipways and building stone walls! Hand cream was hastily added to her shopping list.

'Enough lies, I know my place,' she said ruefully, casting vanity and her dreams into oblivion.

Having given up any hope of looking wonderful, she let her entire face relax. Petra was treated to one of Trish's dazzling grins, her teeth gleaming white in the darkness of her bronze-gold complexion.

'I'll be the one who makes everyone else look elegant and sophisticated,' Trish decided. 'I'll do my bumpkin act and Adam's intended will adore me because I'm such a cute, folksy character.'

Petra gave her an odd look. 'Don't think so, oh, wizened old peasant. It's my guess that Louise is cheesed off with hearing about the sainted Trish. I bet she's tried on a million outfits and is, at this moment, agonising over her appearance, just like you. Ready?'

Stunned into silence by that remark, Trish let Petra lead her to the lift. Adam couldn't have been talking about her...could he? A smirk of pleasure tilted the corners of her wish-softened mouth before she ruthlessly subdued it.

Too late. He'd made his choice. A beautiful, talented and witty partner who knew how to eat and pronounce tagliatelle without hurling it into her lap while she did so. Someone close to his age and on his wavelength, who could program computers, like him, and organise a dinner party for seventy Japanese businessmen while checking the stock market and painting her perfect toenails. Trish groaned at the paragon she was inventing and wished she hadn't let Petra browbeat her into coming.

After her friend's tireless and unrelenting bombardment of letters and phone calls, she had reluctantly agreed to travel up to London and join the family celebration. She was, so her friend had said, virtually family, after lodging with them for two years. And so she had to wish Adam and his fiancée, Louise, all the happiness in the world.

Gloom descended on Trish as she mentally practised her opening remarks. *Hi, Adam! Wonderful party. Congrats. Is*

*this Louise? Mwa, mwa. Love your dress. 'Scuse me, prom-
ised two panting tigers over there I'd hurry back before
they—*

No. Stupid. Too chirpy and revealing—Adam would see
through her pretence of throwaway confidence immediately. He'd look her deep in the eyes with that intense,
melted-toffee gaze...

She found herself trembling, and hurriedly put her mind
to the problem in hand. Hell, what was she going to say?

Petra chattered engagingly as they walked along the
damask-walled corridor towards a pair of imposing ma-
hogany doors and the Garden Suite beyond. It was a luxu-
rious hotel with ankle-wrecking carpets, impressive oil
paintings and antique furniture. All far too beautiful for
Trish to dare sit on or risk touching with her sticky fingers.
And the silver cutlery looked so heavy that she feared she'd
get repetitive strain injury if she tried to wade through the
entire five courses for dinner.

As they swept past vast urns and baroque marble hall
tables groaning under the weight of stiff floral displays,
Trish barely heard a word her friend was saying.

She was too busy keeping her nerves under control and
rattling around the pathetically sparse contents of her brain,
searching for something casual and witty for her opening
lines. Increasingly she longed to turn tail and run like a
frightened rabbit back to her burrow.

Apart from worrying about the effort of keeping a bright,
see-how-I've-forgotten expression on her face the whole
evening, she felt stranded, like a fish out of water. London
had reduced her to wide-eyed silence. It was horribly noisy
and unfriendly—terrifying, even. She'd made a hash of using the underground, and hadn't a clue about tipping taxi
drivers or doormen. Judging by their open-mouthed amazement, she'd funded their children's private education for
life.

City life was all about speed. People spoke faster, their
movements were quick and frantic, as if there wasn't

enough time in the day to get things done. After just two days, she felt edgy and stressed.

But this was Adam Foster's preferred environment. He'd relocated his computer software business from Truro to London four years ago and become a powerful mover and shaker in this alien world. He must love the hectic pace. Perhaps he was hooked on exhaust fumes. A diesel junkie.

Trish bit her lip, encountering the unfamiliar taste of lipstick. She and Adam were from two different planets. Chalk and cheese. Right now, she wanted to be back home where she belonged.

Yet stubborn curiosity kept her heading for the party. She wanted to see him gazing adoringly at Louise. *Needed* to, for her own peace of mind. Then she'd be able to shrug off the lurking feeling of something unfinished and life-changing. Once this party was over, she'd feel capable of making a commitment to her ever-patient boyfriend.

Time would have changed Adam and she'd probably find that he wasn't a patch on the man she'd once idolised. He might be more Cardigan Man than Danger Man. More socks than sex. She'd changed too. After all, she'd been an impressionable eighteen when she'd last seen him.

Seen! Touched, scoured with her tongue, felt her body dissolve during that long, heart-stopping moment when he'd looked at her and murmured her name... Every detail of their coming together was still fresh and hot in her mind, etched like acid on silver.

Only much later, after she'd fled home in agonies of self-recrimination, had she realised that he'd lost control for one reason only. Adam's grief over the loss of his wife two months earlier had made him reach out blindly for someone to hold. She should have realised that.

Darling Christine's death, after five years of battling with cancer of the spine, hadn't been unexpected. But Adam had been too upset even to attend the funeral. Trish sighed. When he'd looked at her longingly, spoken her name and stretched out his hand, the poor man could never have anticipated that she would react as if he'd made a whole-hearted invitation of love!

Never in the whole of her life had she behaved so badly or felt so ill from guilt and shame. Even now, she stumbled on the teetery shoes, knowing she'd never forgive herself.

They had reached the double doors. She was about to come face to face with him.

'Smile!' hissed Petra. 'You'll strip paint off the skirting boards!'

'Cheaper than turps,' she quipped.

But she obeyed because Adam must be happy now, his wife's death merely a sad memory—and he had a loving woman by his side, in his arms... Trish's smile became a little desperate.

Petra flung open the double doors.

Trish had an impression of raised voices, synthetic perfume and sleek heads. A general air of wealth, confidence and nervous energy emanated from everyone in the banqueting room. Ribbons and roses seemed to be everywhere—nothing jolly, like balloons, she noted wryly. Stiff and awkward, she was horribly aware that she stood out in this high-powered crowd because she looked so ordinary.

'Don't leave me!' she said quickly, turning to Petra. But her friend had been swept into the welcoming crowd, casting helpless, backward 'sorry!' looks at her.

As she stood in the doorway, her eyes skittered about, searching for someone a head and shoulders above the rest and who dominated the room with the sheer strength of his personality. But he was nowhere to be seen. Her shoulders tensed. The ordeal was to be prolonged, then.

All around, Trish could hear snatches of conversation, none of which made sense because people were tossing words such as 'gigabytes' and 'disk formatting failure' at each other. She felt like an alien.

'Hello! What a fabulous tan! Have you been skiing?'

A sentence she could interpret! Trish smiled gratefully at the tall and staggeringly beautiful redhead who'd appeared in front of her. She gave an envious glance at the

perfectly cut shoulder-length bob and the fashionably asym-
metrical cream dress that hugged her languid body like liquid, and said politely, 'No. I live on Scilly—'

'Italy!' exclaimed the vision coolly, her green eyes nar-
rowing inexplicably as she scrutinised Trish's face. 'I adore
Italy. How fascinating. What part?'

'The Scilly Isles, not Sicily,' corrected a low, well-loved
voice from the doorway behind her. 'They're in the
Atlantic, twenty-eight miles to the south-west of Land's
End in Cornwall. Five inhabited, if I remember aright, the
other one hundred and forty islands being left entirely to
Nature.' There was a brief, silken pause. 'Rather like the
inhabitants.'

Adam's hand rested on Trish's shoulder. He and the redhead were exchanging words but she didn't hear them. His
power, his warmth flooded through her entire body, releasing her tense muscles immediately and turning them into
fluid. Trish pretended not to recognise his voice. She was
dealing with a sudden fizz of activity inside her head, and
wanted to be perfectly composed when she faced him.

Thanks, Adam, she thought sourly. She was Miss Nature
in person, was she? Hiding her irritation, she forced a smile,
remembering her decision to be a peasant with straw in her
hair and jolly well like it.

'So!' exclaimed the vision. 'This is Trish, then!' There
was a flash of white as Adam moved to the woman's side.
Trish kept her gaze fixed doggedly ahead, a plastic grin on
her face, as the woman added lightly, 'And all this time I
thought she was Italian! You *look* foreign.'

Louise, for that was clearly who it had to be from the
way she hung onto Adam's tuxedo sleeve, was eyeing
Trish's dark colouring as if it were an inferior brand of face
cream. Trish felt crushed by her cool assessment. Clearly
Louise had been expecting an Italian temptress on the lines
of Sophia Loren, not a badly put-together female with mac-
raméd hair.

Hating the little spurts of jealousy which were shooting
up her body, Trish adjusted her smile to a decent wattage

and said, 'I can't oblige you by producing some Italian genes, but *some* of the time my Spanish blood comes out. When I'm excited, for instance...' She went pink and hastened to make her meaning clear. 'When someone annoys me.'

'Any other time your Spanish blood comes out?' enquired Adam in a wickedly teasing drawl.

She still wouldn't look at him. Her heart was pumping too hard and he sounded far too amused by her discomfort. OK, so amuse him. Go for humour; prove you don't give a damn, a little voice was telling her.

'Yes. If I get careless chopping carrots,' she said sweetly.

He laughed. It was lovely to hear him—and astonishing to see Louise's reaction. Her eyebrows were disappearing into her hairline.

'That's not a sound I've heard for a long time,' Louise said, as if she disapproved of frivolity in a mature man. She pointed a sharp, bare shoulder at Adam in accusation.

'I'd forgotten how. Life's been a bit fraught, hasn't it?' Adam murmured. 'Not much time for fun.' Any fool could have heard the irritation lacing his voice.

Aware of a slight tension building between the two, Trish blundered on. 'Gran says I have quite a few Spanish smugglers and shipwrecked Spanish seamen lurking in my genes. My female ancestors made the most of their opportunities.' She wondered if her eye-to-eye stare with Louise was becoming unnatural, bordering on the manic. Nerves made her gibber unthinkingly. 'When you live on an island the size of a dinner plate, you have to grab all the available talent there is.'

Louise's eyes narrowed even more. Too late, Trish realised she'd now suggested that she was out hunting a man, any man, to take back to her lair. Damn! She wasn't any good at this small talk stuff. How crass she was!

'Hello, Trish,' Adam said, laughter enriching his voice. 'Good to see you again.'

With a properly convivial smile, she began to unwind

one of her rehearsed greetings, speaking to his shirtfront which was so close it came over as a white blur.

'Such a long time, isn't it? How we've aged—!'

'Age be damned!' he protested.

Startlingly, she found herself in his masterful arms, the sound of her name filling her head like sweet music, the smell of him heightening her senses and driving the breath from her body. She wanted them to stay like that for ever.

Her eyes closed, all the better to imagine that situation. His lush mouth pressed warmly into each cheek. It seemed his lips lingered a fraction longer than was socially acceptable but she'd mislaid her brain cells so she was probably wrong. Because when he released her he was smiling—not at her, but at Louise.

Her stomach felt as if it had been subjected to a fast descent in a lift. She decided to be stern with herself. What had she been expecting? A dramatic, 'My God! Trish! I claim you as the woman of my dreams! Goodbye, Louise, all is over!'?

It seemed that subconsciously, that was precisely what she *had* been hoping for. His indifference to their clinch really hurt. And she wondered why she kept on wounding herself with so many impossible and downright immoral desires where he was concerned.

She hadn't come to snatch him away, but to beat it firmly into her dim brain that Adam was far too handsome and talented for the likes of her. For heaven's sake, how could she compete with a red-headed goddess who'd been given Adam's seal of approval?

'I'm a little late with the introductions, but as you gathered, Louise—' he said easily '—this is Trish. Trish, Louise, my fiancée.'

'Welcome to our Engagement Party.'

Louise made sure Trish knew that the occasion merited capital letters. A little tenser than before, the woman leant forward and kissed Trish coolly, as if embracing a stranger's child. With the emphasis firmly on *child*.

Trish kept her carefree smile pinned in place. Louise was

far more gorgeous than she'd imagined, even if she didn't know the difference between the Scilly Isles and the island of Sicily. But then, brainy people often lacked common sense and everyday knowledge.

'I'm still puzzled,' Louise cooed, detached from Adam suddenly as four worshipping blondes surrounded him with cries of adoration.

Casting a furtive glance at him, Trish saw them cover him in lipstick in seconds. Surprisingly, Louise seemed impervious to this. Trish itched to drag the women off and berate him for smiling at them. Instead, she made herself pay attention to Louise, suppressing the brief impression she'd had of Adam. He hadn't changed one iota. Still very dark, very handsome, fiercely male. Damn.

'Why are you puzzled?' she asked Louise, trying to care.

'A tan! In England, in early April?' She peered at Trish's skin. 'Sunlamp or fake tan?' she suggested with suspicious innocence.

'Neither! Just sun and wind and rain. Adam said the inhabitants of the Scilly Isles are all children of Nature, remember?' she said, smarting a little from the description. It had taken her an hour to get ready—longer than she'd ever spent on herself before! 'I lead an outdoor life—'

'You run a guesthouse! That's indoors!' Louise stated knowledgeably.

Lord! thought Trish. What had Adam told her? 'Yes, but on my island we don't have transport—there aren't any made-up roads,' she explained patiently. 'We travel by boat. Bryher is only a mile wide and a mile and a half long—'

'Good grief! Some people have gardens larger than that! And did you say no *roads*?' Louise shuddered elegantly and waved her left hand about, so that Trish could be dazzled by the flashing diamond the size of an elderly broad bean on her ring finger. 'Sounds hell! Don't you get horribly muddy going out to dinner and the theatre? Or to the shops?'

'We don't have restaurants apart from the one in the

hotel. There are a couple of cafés.' She grinned. 'No theatres at all. We get the odd liner going aground, and container ships flinging their cargo at us when they're ship-wrecked. Other than that there's no entertainment—unless you count the activities of the seabirds and tourists and the odd sing-song in somebody's house.' Apparently Louise didn't. Trish giggled at the woman's appalled expression and didn't spare her. 'There aren't any shops, but we have a really nice post office,' she said in proud yokel style.

'No...*shops*!' gasped Louise, clearly incapable of imagining life without them.

On the periphery of her vision, Trish could see that Adam was looking at her over the heads of the chattering blondes—and that he was vastly amused. It felt like old times for a moment. They'd enjoyed many a laugh together. Trish's heart started an uncomfortable tattoo against her ribs.

Knowing she had to get used to Adam's future wife, she tried hard to remain just a hick guest who wished them both well. 'Bryher has no space for that kind of thing, Louise. It can't even support a doctor or a pub or a school. We grow our own food or get it from the main island—St Mary's—or have it shipped in from the mainland, so we need to be highly organised. We go in for mail order a lot—'

'Yes. So I see.' There was a meaningful pause while Louise scanned Trish's clearly undesirable dress which shrieked its catalogue origins. 'It sounds like the back of beyond! Adam and I eat out every night. We'd die of boredom on your island! You'd loathe it, wouldn't you, darling?' she said, appealing to the newly released Adam, who was deftly removing lipstick smears with a handkerchief from his hard-cut jaw and, Trish noted indignantly, *across his mouth*! 'It's such a primitive place, where Trish lives!'

Trish felt flattened, her whole way of life summarily dismissed by the woman Adam loved. While Louise began to scrub Adam's cheeks fussily, Trish struggled with a nagging little voice inside her head which was questioning the wisdom of his choice of partner. He was a sophisticated city man, she reminded herself, a dominant male who was passionately involved in computer technology. He too would hate her simple life.

Miserably, she stared at her crippling shoes, phrases about megabytes and function keys being flung about over her head and adding to her sense of alienation. She should never have come.

'Island life has its attractions for certain people,' Adam said, being polite. There was a hard edge of irritation in his voice, though. He was probably longing to chat about giga-bytes instead, she thought forlornly.

Louise reclaimed her prize, slipping an elegant, creamy bare arm around Adam's waist in almost a defensively pos-sessive gesture. As if, mused Trish, she was marking her territory. Trish went pale beneath her tan. Had Adam in-dulged in pillow confessions with his fiancée, listing all the women who'd made a pass at him?

'I know so much about you,' confided Louise in a pussy-cat purr.

Trish's eyes were as round as they could be. She felt Adam's hot-chocolate gaze melting into her flesh. Combined with the guilt, the heat and the noise, it made her head swim.

'Five-nine, eight stone ten, twenty-two, passion for tea bread, chicken-rearing and weepy films?' she hazarded, playing the careless, guileless cookie.

'No!' replied Louise gaily, relaxing as she was meant to. 'How you two met. Something about your leaving school at sixteen and staying at Adam's house in Cornwall, be-cause he and his first wife let out rooms to students.' The silk-tongued Louise looked expectant and Trish realised she ought to say something.

'I stayed two years,' was all she could come up with. Then she felt her cheeks go pink because she'd reminded Adam of the reason she'd left. She was aware that he had stiffened and the pall of silence hung between them accusingly.

Louise seemed impervious to the strained atmosphere and was smugly playing with Adam's signet ring, turning it this way and that to admire the plain gold band and entwined initials. 'I forget what you were studying,' she said. 'Which university did you go to?'

'I didn't mention university—' Adam began irritably, stuffing his hand in his pocket.

'Nothing so grand!' Trish could fight her own battles. In her own way. 'I don't have your brains.' She was pleased at Louise's satisfied little smile.

'I'm sure I told you. Trish came to the mainland for a hotel and catering course in Truro,' Adam said curtly.

Louise smiled at Trish, somehow managing not to disturb the serenity of her face. 'You and Petra must be virtually the same age.'

'She's a year older than me,' Trish agreed. 'We found we had the same sense of humour and we've been friends ever since.' Trish looked about wildly for Petra to rescue her. A friend in need was a friend right here!

'That makes you only a teeny bit older than Adam and Christine's son,' Louise said meaningfully.

Trish knew what she was doing. The pussycat was unsheathing her claws. Louise suspected a take-over bid and was making sure they all knew the situation. Adam's son Stephen was nineteen. The message was clear: Keep off this man of mine. Adam is almost twice your age.

It amazed her that Louise bothered to get her claws out at all. A polyester mouse from a remote island with nowhere to buy sushi or Ralph Lauren was hardly going to turn Adam's head!

Demurely, she nodded. In the absence of such a possibility, she could at least turn the conversation instead. 'Is Stephen here?' she asked politely.

Even he, her old adversary and Prince Pain in the Neck, would be a welcome sight at this moment. She needed an excuse to get away from this ego-destroying conversation.

'Leeds University. Studying medicine,' said Adam shortly.

'Brainy.' Trish looked suitably impressed.

'You nursed, didn't you—in the hospice where Adam's wife was?' Louise persisted.

Adam's tension increased but Trish giggled at the unlikely scenario. 'Me? No! I earned money evenings and weekends working in the kitchens as a skivvy, dropping pans of spaghetti, knocking the chef's hat into the cream of mushroom soup—'

'And kept my wife and everyone else in the hospice in gales of laughter, recounting your mishaps,' Adam said softly. 'You made the last months of Christine's life there bearable.'

There was a deep gratitude in his tone. Louise's green eyes became strangely washed out. Trish realised that Petra was right; Adam's fiancée had heard too much too often about Trish Pearce.

'Nice to have a cheerful little friend of Petra's around,' said Louise patronisingly. Her voice wobbled, reducing the impact of the cutting remark.

Trish shifted uncomfortably, wobbled too, on Petra's diabolical heels, and found herself lurching sideways. Adam grabbed her. Their eyes met. Blazed. Lit fires.

Glittering ebony. Searing sapphire.

No, she thought desperately, wishing the world would level itself out again. She was reading his message incorrectly. He was probably warning her not to rock any boats, not to mention what had happened between them.

'Nearly became intimate with the carpet then!' she cried merrily. 'I've got to take these shoes off before I break an ankle or get a nosebleed from the altitude!'

Reaching down, she yanked off the stilted shoes and straightened up again with them in her hands.

Louise looked startled at such wanton behaviour as Trish waved them in triumph. 'You can't go barefoot here!' she cried in horror, as if it were a social sacrilege.

'I can. I am!' Trish said with a grin. 'My toes were folded underneath my feet like a Japanese geisha's. Another ten minutes and I'd have been launching into a chorus of *Madame Butterfly*.'

'Why?' Louise was frowning, trying to make the connection. Her tone hardened to an icy slash. 'You're not being abandoned by your lover because you're unsuitable, are you?'

Trish's mouth dropped open at the bitchy little dig.

'It was a joke,' Adam said tightly, his eyes glinting. 'Trish makes them all the time. Don't read any more into it.'

The two women studied his closed face thoughtfully. Then Louise turned back to Trish.

'Adam thinks a lot of you,' she said, as if explaining Adam's rebuke. 'You...got him through a bad time.' She seemed unable to leave the subject and was plainly jealous of Trish's involvement with Adam.

'She was incredible,' he replied, before Trish could speak. 'She fussed over me when I came out of my study after a fourteen-hour day—that was when I was trying to build up the business—and had me laughing and relaxed before I even had a drink in my hand.'

'I'm a clown,' Trish said hastily, wondering how Adam could be so insensitive—and Louise so beautiful yet insecure.

'Optimist,' corrected Adam. 'And a wonderful cook. She even coaxed Christine to eat, by presenting food appealingly.' He smiled. 'Or in an amusing way. Do you remember those ridiculous hippo-shaped fish steaks?'

Trish laughed. 'Ridiculous or not, you ate four!' she teased, jabbing him in the chest. Then she felt the frosts of Alaska descending on her from Louise's direction and eased off her sudden familiarity with Adam. 'Sad times bring you together,' she excused hastily. 'Don't imagine I'm Wonder Woman. Far from it! I had more disasters on my catering course than anyone. I'd trot into the ward, tell anyone who'd listen about my latest howler and they'd all laugh. My boyfriend,' she said, deliberately lowering her voice to a loving husk and looking gooey, as though her knees went weak at the thought of him, 'says that's my second-best asset.'

'The first being?' clipped out Adam, with a distinct lack of amusement.

'None of your business,' she retorted spiritedly, without glancing at him. She gave Louise a conspiratorial grin. 'That's between him and me. I've known Tim since we were knee-high to a pair of sea boots,' she explained.

'How quaint. Are you getting married soon?' asked Louise, warming to Trish by the second.

'We thought November, when the visitor season is over,' lied Trish, crossing her bare legs since her fingers were otherwise occupied with Petra's shoes. 'And you?' she managed, determined not to be dog in the manger.

There was a moment's silence. 'Oh, you know how it is. Pressure of work and so on. We'll fix a date when we can,' Louise said with an unconvincing attempt at being offhand. 'We're up over our heads in work. Fall-out from the millennium time bomb, you know. Lord knows when we'll find a nanosecond to organise the wedding, let alone a honeymoon.'

Bombs? Trish didn't know what Louise was talking about. 'It sounds very stressful,' she said sympathetically, thinking wistfully of her island, the slow pace of life, and the endless skies and dancing turquoise seas, so clear that the seabed could be seen through fathoms of water.

Her face had become dreamy, its lush sensuality knife-jacking Adam back to the past. He had kissed those smoke-dark lids, felt the flicker of her thick black lashes beneath his lips, held that strong and work-lean body in his arms and marvelled at the sexual energy trapped there...poised, waiting eagerly for him to unleash it.

A surge of passion ripped through his body, startling him with its intensity. He all but shook from the effort of not grabbing her, throwing her over his shoulder, storming up to his room and making mad, reckless love to her till he'd got her out of his system.

Shocked by the unexpectedness of his arousal, he invented a polite excuse and latched onto the party organiser, close by. It took several minutes of boring chit-chat about canapés and staff problems before his desire receded. Finally he felt able to walk again.

With a practised ease, he ended the chat and strode purposefully away, not stopping until he had left the party and was safe in the cool darkness of the walled Victorian garden. Leaning back against the smooth bark of a plane tree, he lifted his head to the night sky, his eyes dark and brooding as guilt and fury possessed him in equal measures.

Louise had been rude: unnecessarily cutting and superior. It was a side of her he'd never seen before. And Trish had dealt with it in her usual generous, tolerant way. Just as well. He would have sprung to her defence otherwise.

So it wasn't finished, then. He frowned.

There were no stars in the vast, velvet canopy. The city lights cast too strong a glow. But he knew they were up there. Seeing Trish again—radiant and beautiful, with that appealing inner sweetness and the humour which made him glad to be alive—had wiped away the veils which had obscured his vision. She'd sparkled like a star in that room. Unique, dazzling, soul-lifting.

But he had no business to be thinking of her. This occasion was his public commitment to Louise. He was acting like a barbarian with his brains in his trousers! Hell, he despised himself!

He needed to take some action. Drag Louise off to bed, maybe? His wry grin eased his tension slightly. Louise would be appalled if she couldn't take off her make-up beforehand. Whereas Trish...

His eyes narrowed. From the moment he'd woken that terrible morning four years ago, and found she'd gone without saying goodbye, he'd put her out of his mind. It was the way he dealt with strong emotions. In his youth he'd perfected that useful technique. Unknown to him, however, Trish had found a little space in his mind in which to nestle.

And now she was back, filling his every thought with a

vengeance because he knew what an incredible woman she was. Adam felt the hunger for her, the admiration, filling every part of his heart.

The hardness of his mouth softened and his whole body stilled. Trish had played a large part in easing Christine's last moments. Happy, and smiling at something Trish had said, his wife had whispered, 'My love to Stephen... Goodbye, Petra, sweetheart.' Then her voice had faded and he'd just caught her final words: 'Darling!' and 'Love' and 'Trish'. Then she'd slipped quietly away and he'd known that Christine had found peace at last.

At the time he'd wanted to hold Trish in his arms, to thank her with a heartfelt hug. But he'd never dared. Because he'd known very well that there might be more in his regard for her. He had recognised what she could mean to him one day. Besides, she was young, and deserved someone of her own age. It wasn't impossible to keep the lid on his need—or so he'd thought, till that moment when he'd almost made love to her.

Adam scowled, hating himself for his momentary lapse. Turning, he raised his hand to slam it into the tree hard enough to hurt. At the last minute he controlled his anger and placed his palm carefully on the patterned bark, as if testing his ability to override his feelings by sheer will-power.

He'd had no right to paw her. She was naturally kind and compassionate. He'd read more into her actions than he should have done. She had a good and loving heart which encompassed everyone in her path. Petra, himself, Christine, all the inhabitants of the hospice—And what had he done? Overstepped the mark and scared her off. Clumsy, arrogant fool!

He leant his forehead against the trunk, needing to think, to calm his emotions and to regain his equilibrium. But he didn't have the time. Every second of his life was spoken for. He and Louise had built the company up and now their responsibilities were overwhelming them both. They'd spent so long in the office together that it had made sense to extend their partnership to their non-existent personal lives.

At least with Louise he wouldn't ever be vulnerable. She would never be able to hurt him and he would never lose control of himself. Without warning, his long-buried teen-age memories surfaced and pain tightened his mouth. Ruthlessly he overcame it by crushing his car keys in his hand till he all but cried out. He was damned if he'd let his emotions be tested to destruction again!

A footfall sounded, soft and barely discernible. Looking up, he saw the barefooted Trish making her way thought-fully down the silvered path between shrubs gleaming in the moonlight. His heart leapt and sank in quick succession. Carefully he commanded his racing pulses to subside. And they did.

'Escaping my party?' he accused laconically.

Trish jumped in surprise, looked embarrassed, and then tossed her gloriously shaggy black hair in an appealing ges-ture of freedom which caught so brutally at his heart.

''Fraid so! They're all talking a foreign language in there!' she declared. She remained—to his relief—a safe yard or so from him. 'Cell merge, bullets, and hyper-link... I wanted to scream!'

Adam chuckled. There it was again. Laughter. He felt less hassled already. 'It's a narrow little world,' he admit-ted, reining himself in ruthlessly.

'Like mine,' she conceded, inspecting her perfect honey-coloured toes. 'We really are living on different planets, aren't we?'

He thought at first that she didn't sound too happy about that. But she was smiling brightly, dazzling the darkness with her lovely laughing mouth, so he knew he'd been de-luding himself.

Determined, however reckless that might be, to prolong this brief interlude alone with her, he said wryly, 'My planet's hurtling into chaos.'

She nodded. 'That bomb?' she asked uncertainly, wid-ening her beautiful sapphire eyes. 'I know you'll think I'm stupid, but I didn't understand the reference. You haven't joined the bomb-disposal squad in your spare time, have you?'

Adam wondered if he could—should—spin out the explanation, or cut it short and get back to the party. No contest. Here there was a peace of sorts. And Trish. What the hell?

'I don't have spare time,' he reminded her. 'No, the millennium time bomb is to do with the way some older computers were programmed, especially the large mainframe ones used by councils and corporations.'

He hesitated, disconcerted by her intentness. It was as though she was mesmerised, her huge eyes, beneath that ludicrous fringe, framed by spiky black lashes. Incredibly lovely, he thought, a little lurch of his heart warning him that he must be staring. But he longed to touch each faint laughter line around her sparkling eyes and work out how many laughs it had taken to produce each one.

'Go on,' she said, into the soft night.

To keep his hands from reaching out, he folded his arms firmly across his chest. Her gaze slowly passed over its curve, her lashes fluttering, her mouth emitting a faint sigh. An electric current switched on every nerve in his body. He wanted to kiss those drowsy, parted lips. Run exploratory fingers up the inside curve of her fabulous bare legs. It would take for ever—but it would be a journey worth making.

He sucked in his breath sharply, aware from the straining of his body that he wanted more than that. Appalled, he frowned and tried to drive out all lustful thoughts.

'The date system,' he said briskly, 'was set up on the assumption that it would always be nineteen-something— 1959, 1990, and so on. Suddenly everyone realised the millennium was due and panicked.'

He stopped, running out of breath. Because all he could think about was her lithe, shapely body writhing beneath his hands—

Trish took a few steps closer, her brow furrowed. 'Why?'

'Why?' Yes. Why was he carrying a torch for his step-daughter's friend? he asked himself savagely. He had Louise. Stunning, clever, computer literate... His heart could remain untouched. What more could he want?

'Why did they panic?' she asked, some illusion making her voice sound throaty and infinitely appealing.

'Because,' said Adam curtly, finding it almost impossible to concentrate, 'the systems only pay attention to the last two digits of a date. So to the computer the year 2000 means zero-zero. In other words, back to 1900 again.'

She gurgled with delighted laughter, her eyes twinkling with fun. 'We'll all have to leap into hansom cabs and celebrate the relief of Mafeking! How lovely! Technical experts thrown into a muddle! Oh. Sorry, Adam. That includes you, doesn't it?'

'Certainly does! And I've been trying to sort out the mess. It would be funny,' he agreed with a crooked smile, 'if it hadn't meant that some people's pensions weren't going to be paid out—because according to the computer they wouldn't have been born!'

'Oh, dear! What a muddle!' she said with a frown, as if she really cared about people she'd never met. But that was Trish all over.

An urge to kiss her open mouth and plunder its depths forced him to stare vaguely over her head. 'Megabyte size,' he agreed. 'My company's been flat out re-programming for the past few years. Our priority has been ensuring the smooth running of airlines and railways and other essential services. Without re-programming, they would have ground to a halt.' Shaking from sexual tension, he passed a hand through his hair, dislodging the cow-lick, which was normally severely repressed. 'It's been a race against time itself. We've been working sixteen-hour days for as long as I can remember and we're still picking up the pieces.'

She sighed. 'You look like you need a holiday.'

'Is that an offer?' he asked quietly, before he could stop himself.

There was a pause, as if he'd confused her and she

couldn't think of a polite answer. Her cheeks looked pinker beneath the tan and he realised that she was thinking of a polite way to discourage him. She'd already fled once from his unwelcome advances.

'On my island? In my guesthouse? Louise was right. You'd hate it,' she said, her expression distinctly ice-packed. 'It's very small. Two doubles, one single. No, I see you in some vast, swanky hotel in the Seychelles—'

'Lounging on a beach?' he asked incredulously, his eyes hard and cynical as he dealt with her rejection.

'No. Not you.' Her neat teeth briefly pulled at her plush lower lip. 'Louise will be sunbathing in a fabulous bikini and you'll be making everyone furiously envious of your water-skiing technique. Or paragliding. Or snorkelling.'

He frowned, taken aback by her perception. She had described the brief working holiday they'd had in Florida a few months ago. It had been something of a disaster.

What *would* he and Louise do in their leisure hours together? They'd never had any real free time, so it hadn't occurred to him before how they'd fill it. She occasionally dashed out shopping for clothes; they ate hastily in the best restaurants and fell into bed—separately. They both fitted in their personal training sessions before breakfast and he couldn't remember when they'd last indulged in a spontaneous passionate clinch.

Honour made him fight to hold onto the promises he'd made to his fiancée.

'I thought honeymoons were for non-stop sex,' he said shortly, giving himself a point from which there was no return.

Trish winced, as if his directness was in bad taste. Which it was. But he needed to convince himself that he was doing the right thing this time. Her arms came protectively around her body as though she needed to defend herself from his coarseness.

Whereas she was more in danger of being kissed till neither of them could breathe. The moonlight gleamed on the proud Spanish bone structure of her face and shimmered alluringly along her shapely arms. Her defensive gesture had lifted her breasts and they were thrusting against the smooth emerald material. She must be cold, he thought dazedly, because her nipples had hardened into tempting peaks. There was something soft and vulnerable about her expression and he had never wanted anyone more.

God help him! He was sick in his mind. Perverted in his body. Louise was the woman he wanted, had pursued... No. She had pursued him. Made herself indispensable. Become part of his life, apart from his bed.

Maybe that was it. He was sex-starved. Relieved, he gave Trish a slightly sardonic smile and she wilted before him, then rallied.

'Not non-stop,' she said earnestly. 'I agree that honeymoons are traditionally supposed to be the month after your marriage when you drink nothing but mead and—'

'Do what?' he asked, startled.

'Mead. Honey. Where do you think ''honeymoon'' came from? Mead's an aphrodisiac—'

'I wouldn't need it,' he said with deliberate cruelty.

Her mouth thinned. 'I'm sure.' There was a moment's awkward silence. Then she sucked in a breath and launched into speech as if she felt driven by compulsion. 'There's more to it than that, though! Honeymoons are for getting to know the person beneath the skin!' she added vehemently. 'Enjoying being in the same room. Finding pleasure in doing little things for each other—'

'Trish!'

In his attempt to control his voice, he'd sounded harsh and angry. Amazed by her almost incoherent outburst, he stared at her. Longing to drink mead with her for the rest of his life. Adoring her passion and envying her uninhibited surrender to her emotions. Duty and responsibility holding him fast.

'Sorry. I got carried away. I've no idea why. Champagne in my veins instead of blood, I suppose! I—I'm sure you love Louise in all those ways,' she said huskily.

All he could think of was a sudden linking in his mind

of Christine's words. 'Love…Trish.' But he kept his inner
thoughts masked by a cold and unfriendly expression.

'Louise and I are perfectly suited,' he said with convic-
tion.

'That's lovely.'

With her slender jaw set in hard lines, she gave a little
grimace of a smile, turned and walked out of his life.

CHAPTER TWO

TRISH ran into the kitchen and flung down the flowers she'd been picking in the cottage garden. Then she reached out to open the oven door a crack to check the Dundee cake, her other hand grabbing the ringing phone.

'Hi, Trish! It's me! Petra! What happened to you?'

Adam had happened!

She closed the oven up. 'Sorry I bolted. I was worried about Gran, all alone next door. But mostly I hated London,' she said, shamefaced. 'I didn't have anything to say to anyone at the party so I stopped boring everyone with my yokel act, packed my polyester dress and took the sleeper back to Penzance. Caught the morning helicopter. Got back home a few hours ago. Sorry, Pets. I was going to call you when I got a moment.'

'You rushed off without warning once before, duckie. Adam seems to be the common factor.'

Her friend was too sharp by half! 'Nonsense! I get home-sick.'

'Yeah.' There was a sceptical pause. 'You haven't got another runaway there, have you?'

Trish gently slid a tray of waiting flapjacks onto the shelf below the Dundee. 'No, only me, Gran and the chickens. Gran's watching my exhausted video of *Dirty Dancing* and the chickens are guzzling their greens.' She reached into the fridge for the tea bread. 'Why?'

'Adam's gone missing,' Petra said casually.

The plate in Trish's hand clattered to the floor. 'What... what...?' Confused, she thanked her lucky stars the plate had landed right side up and the bread was intact. 'You're joking!' she cried, fascinated.

'Nope. Vanished some time in the early hours. Left a note saying a job had come up. Forgot to leave a contact

34

number and his mobile's switched off. Louise is hopping
mad. I wondered if he'd got sick of the rat race and booked
in to your isolated pig-house.'

'It's a lovely stone cottage in an idyllic setting and you
know it. You've been four times—it can't be that bad,'
Trish retorted with a grin. 'As a matter of fact, I do have
a last-minute booking which came ten minutes after I'd set
foot in the door this morning, but—'

'Who?' squeaked Petra excitedly.

'Oh, put your hat back on. Nobody exciting. It's a Mr
Rowe. Mack Rowe.'

There was a choking sound on the end of the line.
'Macro!' Petra said eventually, her voice distorted by a
mass of giggles.

'What's up with you?' demanded Trish suspiciously. 'Is
someone tickling you?'

'I should be so lucky! Gotta go! Give Macro my love—'

'Don't be silly, Pets,' Trish said fondly. 'He doesn't
know you from Adam.'

A squeal of laughter ricocheted down the line. Trish realised what she'd said and began to giggle, too.

'I'll be in touch,' jerked Petra, in fits of laughter. 'Bye!'

With no time to wonder if her friend was cracking up at
last, Trish prepared the best guest room. Vases of flowers,
home-made biscuits in a tin, orange and cinnamon soap and
bath oils ready in the *en suite*, magazines, soft, fluffy tow-
els... She looked at the chintzy bedroom proudly, then she
went to finish the vegetables for the evening meal and to
set up a welcoming tea tray.

Trundling down to Church Quay in her borrowed hill
buggy, with terns calling overhead and the scent of honeysuckle filling her nostrils, she reflected that it was just as
well Adam wasn't interested in her. He'd never give up
city life with all its attractions, and she'd never give up
Bryher.

It was still hard, though, coming to terms with the aching
sense of loss she'd had, ever since she'd stolen out of the
hotel like a thief in the night. She was glad to be busy.

From past experience she knew that if she worked non-stop and fell into bed exhausted she'd have less time to feel sorry for herself.

The thought of going home had instantly lifted her spirits. As the train had gathered speed, London's concrete and tarmac had melted away into the distance. Green fields and trees had flashed by the window and her aching heart had been soothed a little.

She'd even hugged herself when Land's End came into sight. The end of England. Nothing ahead but the Scilly Islands, scattered like glittering jewels in the vast Atlantic. Together with the tourists on board the helicopter, she'd looked down on the dramatic jagged rocks and Caribbean-white beaches with enormous excitement.

It was good to be home. Tim might not make her feel ecstatic—and they didn't see one another often, as he lived on the main island. But they were terribly fond of one another. Her future lay with him.

Her decisions made, Trish drove onto the soft white sand by the quay in quite a cheery frame of mind. Parked there already was the Land Rover which belonged to the only hotel on the island. She chatted with Norman, its driver, and watched the afternoon boat from Tresco island heading towards them.

Trish and Norman wandered along the quay to meet their guests. She greeted Bryher's handful of schoolchildren, smart in their royal-blue sweatshirts, coming home after a day at Tresco Island School. They scrambled off the *Faldore* with an ease born of a lifetime spent getting in and out of boats. Trish watched them skipping and running happily to their parents. They were followed by a small group of holiday-makers—

And Adam.

She stood on the quay, dumbstruck. He wore what he probably assumed was suitable casual wear: beige linen trousers and a shirt and matching V-neck the colour of samphire leaves. But everything was too clean and pressed. He was far too well groomed to fit in. This was a city man to the core. In comparison with the other visitors, in their walking boots, well-worn jeans and sweatshirts, he looked totally out of place.

He put down his cases, smiled faintly and raised his eyebrows in query, as if his presence was the most natural thing in the world. Reluctantly she walked towards him. *He intended to stay!*

Frantically she looked around for Norman, to take Adam off her hands and sweep him away to the hotel. But Norman seemed content with his quota of guests and was already stacking luggage into the back of the Land Rover.

'Hello!' she said, summoning up a cheery tone for Adam's benefit. 'You'd better hurry! You'll miss your lift to the Hell Bay Hotel!'

'I'm not staying there.'

It was the way he looked at her that made the penny drop. Dismay flooded her face. 'Oh, no, Adam! No! You're not... You can't be...Mack Rowe—!'

'Macro.' His features had tightened slightly at her groan. 'It's a computer term, Trish. I hoped you wouldn't recognise it.'

Petra had known, she thought, furious with her friend for not warning her. So she was to give Petra's love to Macro, was she? Her eyes blazed with anger.

'*Why?*' she forced out fiercely.

He didn't seem too pleased at her lack of enthusiasm. 'Because you wouldn't have given me house room, would you?'

Her expression told him he'd hit the nail on the head with marksman-like accuracy. 'You had no right to deceive me!' she said hotly.

'Needs must,' he replied, his jaw set like granite. 'I don't let anything stand in my way. I had to be here; I made sure that happened.'

'It didn't sound like you on the phone,' she muttered crossly.

'It wasn't. A colleague fixed it up.'

'But...' She had to ask. Defying his alarmingly linked

dark brows, she looked him straight in the eyes and asked incredulously, 'You're here on business?'

'What else?' he replied crisply, picking up his Louis Vuitton and a black leather briefcase. 'The hotel's full. I thought of you.'

'But...apart from the hotel, there's no one on Bryher with a computer worthy of your personal attention—'

'How do you know?'

She gave him a pitying look. 'Because everyone on the island knows everyone else's business!'

'Why shouldn't there be someone in one of the self-catering cottages who needs expert help?'

'Someone important enough to drag you here?' she demanded.

'It would have to be, wouldn't it?'

'Oh.'

Bemused, she stood staring at him, transfixed by the thought that Adam was here, on her island. Her gaze moved to his smooth jaw and throat. He swallowed at the same moment that she did. Hastily she flicked her eyes to the high line of his broad shoulder. He was tense.

Perhaps he was worried that he'd be left to sleep on the beach, she thought wryly, her confused eyes meeting his.

'Are you going to leave me here to fend for myself, as a punishment for playing a trick on you?' he drawled.

'I'm tempted. You deserve to be tied up and left to sleep in the kelp pit!'

'Kelp. That's seaweed, isn't it?' he asked uncertainly.

'Yes.'

He arched one sardonic eyebrow. 'I'd be very smelly.'

She tipped up her chin. 'That would be the least of your problems. You'd probably die of exposure before anyone could complain.'

A faint smile eased Adam's hard mouth. 'Nice to be given island hospitality.'

Trish felt ashamed. 'I suppose you'll have to stay with me,' she said grudgingly. 'How long are you planning on working here?' She glanced at her hands in surprise. They were trembling. 'Your colleague said up to a week.'

Her breath had shortened. A week! In the same house as Adam again, serving him breakfast and dinner, cleaning his room, touching his things! She'd be a bag of nerves.

'Depends,' he said cryptically. 'I'll pay for two weeks in advance, just to keep the room, as a precaution. I should have got the problems sorted out by then.'

'Two...' Trish's eyes glazed. Luckily her hair was blowing over her face so he probably didn't notice that she was in a state of shock.

'You'll hardly know I'm around. Where's your car?' He shaded his eyes and followed the progress of the Land Rover till it disappeared around the corner by the church. 'I thought you said there was no transport?'

Dazed, she motioned for him to follow her to the beach. 'We only use vehicles to collect and return people who have luggage. And to pick up stores,' she said faintly. Glum-faced, she strode towards the buggy. There wasn't another boat till the morning, but maybe she could persuade him to take it. 'I borrow the ATV—the all-terrain vehicle— from the neighbouring flower farm. I bake a cake or two in return. For the rest of the time, we walk. Adam, I think you'd be better off on Tresco. Or the main island, St Mary's. Bryher isn't your sort of place at all, and if you've business here you can commute each day—'

'I have to be on Bryher,' he said firmly. 'Wait a minute.'

He dumped his bags and walked to the edge of the water. It lapped at his city loafer-shod feet in gentle, almost imperceptible waves. The narrow and treacherous waters between Bryher and Tresco islands had never seemed so sparkling and clear. The deep turquoise sea was far more beautiful to Trish than anything the Pacific had to offer.

Adam made a leisurely three-hundred-and-sixty-degree turn, drinking in the wild and rugged rocks, the unspoilt beach with its specks of mica glinting like metal, and the small green hills. She watched the tension draining from him and found herself smiling. The wind was toying with his hair and he looked very young suddenly, as if the island had already worked its magic on him.

'It's…' He held out his hands in a helpless gesture. She waited for his verdict, her breath suspended. 'Idyllic.'

'Not in winter,' she countered, yet felt pleased, despite her decision to deter him from staying more than a night. 'Hell Bay didn't get its name for its placid nature, you know. We get the full fury of Atlantic gales and mountainous seas. Sometimes we're trapped on the island because the boats can't get out—'

'Are you politely trying to put me off, Trish?' he asked, a sardonic smile playing about his lips.

She scowled. 'Put your luggage in the trailer,' she said sharply. 'I'm merely setting the record straight. I hate it when visitors come and decide it's paradise here, on the basis of a few sunny days. To love Bryher, you have to experience the storms, which tear your roof off and hurl seawater and sand over your house and ruin your sprouts! OK, you can laugh, but it's serious when your fresh veg are spoiled! You need to face the hardship, all the drawbacks—and yet still love it unconditionally.'

'Like in a marriage.' He lifted both cases into the back of the ATV.

There had been significance in that remark. She shot him a quick look, trying to judge what he was up to.

'I imagine you'd know about that,' she said testily, failing to muster a smile of indifference. 'After working together for so long, you and Louise must know each other better than most old married couples.'

Adam's eyes were searching the ground so she couldn't see his reaction. He bent and picked up a small tower shell and a wentletrap. He spent a while examining the whorls and ridges before slipping the two shells into his suit pocket.

'I feel out of place, standing here in these clothes,' he said with a rather forced laugh. 'Shall we go? I'd like to change into something more suitable.'

Trish hesitated, loath to invite him to ride the buggy with

her. He could stand on the bar behind the single seat, but
that would mean having his arms around her waist. She
swung a jean-clad leg over the saddle, hiding her amusement as he searched in vain for somewhere to sit.

'Right. Follow the track...' she began.

'You mean I'm walking?' he asked in amazement.

She gave him a pitying glance. He probably did all his
walking on a machine in a gym. 'Toddlers can do it. I think
you'll find it comes back to you after a while,' she said
sarcastically. 'You can't get lost. Up the hill, then down to
the bay. Kelp Cottage is on the beach. Come in the green
door. The scarlet one with flowers painted on it is Gran's.
You won't want to meet her till I've primed you about her
funny ways.'

Before he could protest, she'd roared off, kicking up
clouds of sand. She felt sure he'd miss the benefits of civilisation long before the end of the week. He seemed uncomfortable, as if he knew he didn't fit in. He was a fish
out of water, just as she'd been in London, and he'd soon
get bored and leave. Till then she'd have to cope with her
reaction to having him around.

She'd treat him like a normal guest. Good food, loaves
of home-made bread and a decent wine, plus a relaxed and
friendly manner. Why should she swan about looking
tragic, like Greta Garbo, just because she was struggling
with some stupid infatuation?

Adam watched her go, his eyes full of affection, the corners
of his mouth tight with regret. Emotions he'd never known
he'd possessed were waging a war within him.

His sole purpose in coming was to rid himself of Trish
for ever so that he could get on with his chosen path in
life. Since meeting her at the party, he thought about making love to her all the time. What he needed was to be
rejected so conclusively that his brain and his body got the
message. If he pushed her enough, perhaps made a pass,
he reckoned she'd get snappy, bitchy and lose her temper.

So of necessity he was being devious. What he was about

to do would hurt his pride like hell. Rejection had only figured once in his life and it had messed him up for years. But the alternative—launching into a relationship with Trish—would be worse.

Far better to be spared the disastrous outcome of any stupid behaviour. Like imagining she and he could be lovers. Or that he might fancy living with her on a small lump of granite in the Atlantic Ocean.

He grinned. The implications of falling in love with Trish were too appalling to contemplate!

The buggy vanished around a bend in the lane. He set off across the sand and began the gentle climb past the squat church, swallows swooping over his head, competing with the evocative cries of the gulls. And then they were gone.

A deep silence fell. Honeysuckle smothered the tumbled stone walls beside the track, scenting the warm air with dizzying perfume. He passed tiny fields, smaller than tennis courts, hedged to a height of ten feet and blazing with tall purple flowers. The distant thrum of an outboard engine joined the lazy drone of bees, the distant wash of waves on a shore.

His mobile phone burred softly. He'd left it on line after using it on Tresco Island. Out of habit, his hand strayed to the slim holster on his belt and then checked. The sound seemed sacrilegious out here. With a decisive gesture, he slid the phone from the holster, disabled it and replaced it again. Now no one could reach him. He might as well be adrift on a boat, or marooned on a desert island.

Adam let out a long-held breath. And with it went a good deal of the tension which had knotted his muscles for the past year or so and given him daily headaches. The air was crystal-clear like champagne and he felt like running, laughing, letting go of all the things that weighed him down.

'Magic,' he murmured, when he crested the hill.

He could see right across the island, the bay he'd just left on one side, a new one on the other. Glittering granite rocks littered the mouth of this sandy cove, giving it a film-set appearance. Beyond were dozens of small islands and above him wheeled elegant black and white birds, assailing his ears with a strange, piping call. This was Trish's home. She'd described it often enough, but the reality left him breathless.

Invigorated, he strode towards the rose-covered cottage on the beach. He felt less depressed. And, given his self-inflicted task, couldn't for the life of him understand why.

'Enjoy your walk?' asked Trish provocatively.

'Very much,' he said, to her surprise. 'What are the tall purple flowers in those doll-sized fields called?'

'Whistling Jacks—a kind of gladioli. They come up after the narcissi. We sell them on the mainland. The hedges protect them from the gales.'

'I see. And there were some black and white birds—'

'With a red beak and eye? Oyster-catchers.' She looked at him curiously. He seemed very interested for a city man.

Adam looked impressed. 'It was fascinating, walking up that lane. I suppose you know the names of all those peculiar-looking plants. Those giant ones, for instance.' He grinned. 'Twelve feet tall with blue flowers?'

'Echiums,' she said promptly. 'We can grow a lot of exotic plants because we rarely have frost or snow.'

Adam's face was soft with pleasure. 'I haven't been so close to wildlife for years. I envy your knowledge.'

She liked his admiration and basked in it for a moment before she said, 'I know about my world, you know about yours. You think it's clever to know the names of birds and plants I've lived with all my life. I goggle at anyone who knows computer-talk as well as plain English.' Suddenly she felt that they were getting too cosy and decided to end their chat. 'I've taken your luggage upstairs,' she said, mustering a more impersonal tone.

'Trish! You shouldn't have done that!' he protested at once.

'Don't go all macho on me!' She grinned, incapable of

remaining aloof for long. 'I'm as strong as Rambo,' she told him, flexing her biceps like a body-builder. 'I'm not fragile and feminine like Louise.'

He appeared to be about to contradict her, then changed his mind. 'She's tough in a different way,' he said.

Hard as nails, thought Trish, uncharitably. She frowned at her tart jealousy and vowed to think well of his fiancée.

'Anyway, you're a guest here. My job is to look after you,' she said. 'Perhaps I'd better show you around. That's the sitting room in there...'

He peered at the cheerfully cluttered room with its comfortable chintz chairs, rows of bookcases and the incomparable view of jagged islands in the sapphire sea.

'Sunny aspect. I'll enjoy sitting in there with you,' was his verdict.

'I'm usually busy baking in the evenings,' she said quickly. 'You'll have to watch *Coronation Street* on your own.'

'I rarely get to see any TV,' he said, with a smile at her cheeky put-down. 'I usually work in the evenings too.'

'Poor Louise!' she murmured sympathetically, leading him through to the conservatory at the back.

'She works alongside me.'

Trish suppressed her involuntary flinch. 'Great for intimacy.'

'I'll say,' he replied enthusiastically.

Her lips compressed for a moment, then she remembered that he was a paying guest, nothing more.

'I've laid on tea for you.' On her best welcoming behaviour, she pulled out the white wicker chair. 'You have breakfast in here, squeezed in between the geraniums and petunias. Or outside, if it's warm enough. Dinner ditto.'

'Wonderful,' he said, when she'd expected him to turn his nose up at the cramped conditions.

'I'll go and make the tea and bring tonight's menu,' she continued pleasantly. 'Help yourself to tea bread. The flapjacks and Dundee cake were made today. Any preferred brand of tea?'

'Earl Grey with lemon.' He seemed to be fighting down laughter. 'Join me, Trish. And stop being so damn formal!'

'You're getting the same treatment as anyone who comes here!' she said indignantly. 'I can't deviate from the script—I'd forget something!'

She left him laughing, and as she put the kettle on to boil she knew she was longing to be on easy terms with him again. Should she sit with him or not? There were a thousand jobs she could be doing. Her conscience and desires had a brief tussle. One cup of tea—just to be friendly, she decided, pleased with her cool compromise.

Surrounded by tumbling passion flowers and scarlet geraniums, and with jasmine shedding petals on his head, Adam had stretched out his legs and was finishing a sticky slab of tea bread. He slowly licked his fingers, his eyes fixed on the garden but his mind miles away. On Louise, Trish supposed. Then a small curl of erotic pleasure tweaked at her breasts as he sucked his forefinger in very sexy contemplation.

'Right! Tea!' she cried merrily, as though she were producing vintage champagne. 'I can only stop a moment. The weeds in the garden are in danger of taking over the whole island!'

Adam's rich chuckle warmed her body. 'It's an amazing place! Like a jungle!' he said, leaning forward in admiration, as if he were seeing it for the first time.

Flattered, Trish nevertheless felt a pang. He *had* been mooning over Louise. He was missing his fiancée already.

Subdued by this, she poured the tea then took a golden flapjack, noticing that he'd removed his sweater and had rolled his sleeves up to the elbow. His bare, oak-coloured arm lay along the edge of the chair, close to hers. An inch more and they'd be touching.

Something drastic happened to her throat. She began to choke.

'Hold on!'

Adam leapt up and banged her on the back. Her coughing fit ceased but he continued to massage either side of her spine. She let him. A deep warmth invaded her body through the thin T-shirt, loosening tendon, muscle and sinew. The massage became slower. She could hear him breathing. Every inch of her was aware of him and tingling with an electric tension. A light touch of something—his fingers, perhaps?—brushed the nape of her neck and then he was moving back to his chair.

'OK?' he asked abruptly.

No. Aroused. Angry. Resentful... 'Thanks to you. Good thing you were here!' she said vigorously, in an effort to drive the devils from her body. 'Think how awful it would be, having "Suffocation from home-made flapjack" on your death certificate!'

He managed a thin smile at her panic-stricken joke. 'Like me in the kelp pit, I don't think you'd be in a position to care,' he observed drily.

He watched while she cut him a piece of Dundee cake and slid it onto his plate. Quickly she drank her tea and replaced the floral cup in its saucer.

'There. I ought to go—'

'Tell me about the garden first,' he said quietly, gazing out at the wilderness of feathery tamarisk, cistus, daturas, lilies and shrub roses, all competing desperately with herbs and vegetables for a decent space. 'I imagine your mother had a hand in it?'

Sinking back in her seat, Trish smiled gently, touched that he should remember that her late mother had become a gardener in the famous exotic gardens on Tresco. What she hadn't told him, though, was that they'd needed the money because her father had walked out, shortly after she was born.

Her smile faltered. Mainland people like her father often found it hard to adapt to island life. He'd tried to settle, but couldn't bear the isolation.

'I'm sorry,' Adam said, seeing her troubled expression. He reached out his hand as if to touch her arm and then seemed to think better of it. 'I didn't mean to bring back sad thoughts.'

'We've all got tragedies in our lives, haven't we? You
have to learn to live with the sadness.'

'Or bury it,' he said, his voice quiet and very low.

'Oh, no! That means you don't remember the good
times,' she said, aching to see his blank expression.

'I never thought of it like that.' He fell silent.

Trish felt sad. If he was refusing to think of Christine
because the memories hurt, then he was missing some wonderful moments they'd shared.

'I remember only the happiness Mum and I had together,' she said gently, throwing crumbs out to the gathering thrushes. 'She died very peacefully. The iris and fox-
gloves were in bloom and early sweet peas were filling her
room with perfume. She had no money but she's left me a
wonderful legacy, Adam: love and fond memories and the
garden. I think of her every time I walk in it.'

He said nothing in response but he'd relaxed and seemed
absorbed in hand-feeding the thrushes. So she chattered on.

'There was just a field here at first. Mum planted pittos-
porum all round it for protection and then stuffed everything in it she could lay her hands on. She was a very
passionate person, over the top. Not a bit like me!'

There was a tension in the atmosphere between them.
When she cast a sideways look at him, she saw he was
studying her intently, his eyes as dark as rich chocolate, his
mouth infinitely inviting.

'Pass the menu,' he said softly.

She flushed. She'd been talking too much. 'Here it is.
Take your time choosing,' she said stiffly. 'All the meat's
organic. The fish was caught this morning. The veg are
mine.' She got to her feet. 'I'll be in the garden. Let me
know what you want, then you can get on with your business.'

'When's dinner?' he asked, watching her with lazy
amusement.

'Seven-thirty. You help yourself to drinks in the dining
room first and there'll be some home-made nibbles.'

'Sounds tempting,' he murmured, his smile wickedly carnal. He held her gaze for a moment or two, then suddenly said, 'Will you nibble with me?'

It was the sort of remark which should have made her giggle. But she had to turn her back on him and pretend to be dead-heading a scarlet abutilon. All she could think of was his mouth working its way up her body, sliding over her thighs while she moaned in hunger. Nibbles had never seemed so desirable.

'I always drink with the guests,' she said with brittle politeness, appalled by her dangerous feelings for a committed man. 'I hope you know *your* role. You tell me every detail of your day and show me the souvenirs you've bought and bore me rigid about your job. I look interested, try not to let my eyes glaze over and worry about the soup burning.'

'Sounds cosy.'

She flung him a look over her shoulder, suspecting him of mockery. But his expression was unreadable. 'Depends on the guest. See you in a minute or two when you've chosen,' she said edgily, making for the garden door.

'You forgot to give me my key... To let myself in?' he added, when she looked puzzled.

Trish smiled faintly. 'You don't need keys here. I don't think one exists for the cottage. We don't lock our doors. There's no crime, no vandalism. Just clean air and—'

'Women of Nature,' he muttered, under his breath.

Trish suppressed her desire to live up to that idea and uninhibitedly fling off all her clothes and slide her body against his. It was his fault, she thought crossly, furiously twisting off several perfect blooms of an unsuspecting ginger lily. He *would* stand there exuding pheromones!

'No. Clean air and bird droppings,' she corrected him, deliberately bringing herself down to earth.

'Ever the joker,' he drawled. 'I'm beginning to get the message, Trish.'

'What—message?' she enquired as casually as possible.

'About the lack of crime.' He seemed innocent. But then, with Adam, you never could tell.

She relaxed, then tensed again. He had come unnervingly close to her and was fixing her with his dark, come-to-bed gaze.

'Well, it's totally safe here,' she said, feeling anything but.

'So I gather from when they dropped me at the quay on Tresco. I was told that the boat would be arriving in an hour. I was staggered when they told me to leave my luggage by the café wall and go off for a walk!'

Mesmerised by his lazy stare, Trish tried to swallow, failed, and finally succeeded in bypassing the lump of cotton wool in her throat.

'Did you?' she husked, her eyes a startling blue.

He came closer still. Inches separated them. She didn't move away. That would betray her fear of contact. It seemed her body was reaching up to him, every nerve straining for his touch, drawn by an irresistible pull.

'No. My city chains tied me,' he said, very softly. 'I couldn't conceive of leaving my irreplaceable computer bag so I stayed with it. I made back-to-back calls on my mobile and eyed everyone suspiciously if they came within a hundred yards of my luggage.'

She was having difficulty paying attention to what he was saying. His speech had sounded slow and slurred. She had watched his lips moving, fascinated by their sensual curves as they'd shaped each word. And now they were parted over his strong white teeth as though he wanted to...

Her nails dug into her palms, shocking her into reality. 'I hope you called Louise,' she said sharply.

'I left a message on her answering machine.'

'Saying where you were.'

A gleam came into his eyes. 'No. I don't think she'd be too pleased. Do you?'

To her fevered mind, his gaze caressed her lovingly. Her skin felt alive. She was trembling again. Slowly it dawned on her that Adam had recognised Louise's jealousy. He must have wondered about it...or put two and two together. Her eyes closed in brief dismay and she turned away.

Adam knew how she felt about him! Apparently her fascination had been obvious at the engagement party. She might as well have waved a placard announcing the fact, instead of trying to hide her feelings!

'She seems to think I'm a threat,' she said, with a can-you-believe-it laugh.

'But you're not, are you?' he murmured, a strong thread of caution underlying his low tone.

This was a warning, she thought, glad that he stood behind her and couldn't see her shamed face. He wanted her to know that she must abandon any stupid hopes where he was concerned. Only then could she and Petra meet up with him and Louise in the future, for jolly family occasions at Christmas…attend his wedding…

'How could I be a threat?' Bravely she turned, shocked to find herself inches from Adam's body. He remained where he was, his face set hard as a rock. 'Look at me!' she cried shakily, with a self-deprecating laugh.

It was tinged with pain. She didn't want to be unattractive to him. But she had to remind herself that she was.

'I'm looking,' he muttered, frowning in annoyance.

Somehow she met his brooding eyes, certain that he must be anxious about her emotions. 'I have no illusions about myself, Adam,' she said firmly. 'Gran cuts my hair—though I ruined the fringe all on my own. I wear no make-up, I haven't any flattering clothes and I am a stranger to your world. Louise, on the other hand, has it all.'

His eyes glittered, as hard as granite. 'Oh, she has. Beauty, sophistication, grace, social skills—'

Trish laughed. It was that or wince at his eulogy and she had no intention of betraying herself again. 'OK, OK! Don't make me feel *too* inadequate!'

The back of his hand stroked her golden satin cheek. It was a shockingly unexpected gesture that drove the breath from her body.

'Inadequate?' He looked at her strangely. 'But you are beautiful.' His hand fell to his side and his voice flattened. 'In your own way.'

'My, you really know how to flatter a girl, don't you?'
she joked, nursing her aching heart. And her battered pride.
She found herself willing him to touch her again, even if
it was only in sympathy.

Amazingly, he did, his hands clasping her arms while
she stood woodenly, forcing herself not to respond and lean
against that hard chest with a sigh of relief.

'What would you do if I did flatter you?' he demanded.
'If I said that you were the most beautiful woman I'd ever
known, the most generous, most tender-hearted...desir-
able?'

There was a little catch in his voice, as though he found
such claims to be preposterous, and his eyes crinkled appealingly in what she imagined must be suppressed laughter.

'I'd faint with amazement!' she said truthfully, keeping
her head for once. 'Roll about on the ground laughing.
Refer you to an optician. Would you mind letting me go,
Adam? I've got work to do!'

Released abruptly, she made her escape into the garden.
Hot with agitation, she attacked all the weeds in sight with
grim ferocity. Had he noticed that she was still wilting
whenever he came near? Did she look as dopey as she felt?
Trish furiously hoed the carrots, repeatedly jabbing at the
soil till all the weeds had been satisfactorily cut off in their
prime.

'Trish.'

Unnerved by the nearness, the vibrating velvet of his
voice, she spun around, flustered, flushed, flashing-eyed.
'What?'

Without a word, he held out the menu. Judging by the
kindling of his eyes, he was laughing inside again, she was
sure. Humiliated, she snatched it from him, determined that
he wouldn't catch her going gooey ever again.

'I'm impressed. It's an amazing choice,' he said admir-
ingly, indicating the menu. 'Given the limitations of island
life, I'm surprised—'

'That we can manage more than stewed limpets and dandelions?' she asked a little sharply. 'I'll do you seaweed on toast, if it'll make you feel authentically deprived!'

Adam grinned. 'I know the quality of your cooking. I'd be a fool not to indulge in its pleasures. So I'd like... Stupid of me! I've forgotten. Let me see...' He came to her side, a friendly hand on her shoulder as he checked the menu again. 'I remember,' he murmured in her ear. 'Asparagus in Stilton sauce, cream of leek and potato soup, lamb noisettes and Bryher strawberries. With a bottle of Rioja. My mouth is watering already.'

Her eyes slanted sideways. His breath whispered on her face, tantalising her lips. His smile reached right through to her heart. And that annoyed her. What was he doing? Did he always flirt in this meaningless way?

'Try to control it,' she said witheringly. 'You'll have no saliva left for digestion. You won't be eating till seven-thirty.'

With deft fingers, he removed geranium petals from her hair, his mouth so close to her cheek that she only had to turn for their lips to meet. Trish doggedly went through her nine times table, getting stuck, as she always did, on nine sevens.

'Some things that one wants,' he mused, his fingers smoothing down the glossy black strands he'd disturbed, 'are all the better if you have to wait for them.'

'Some things you wait for and never get at all,' she muttered, shrugging off his hand irritably.

Wondering how to erase Adam from her mind, she gave up mathematics, rolled up the menu, stuffed it in her pocket and started hoeing vigorously again.

There was something ridiculous about her fierce and totally unnecessary tilling of the soil. She was desperate to get rid of him. Her last remark had been evidence of that. Yes, OK, he'd wanted her rejection. And he was getting it in spades.

Yet his plan wasn't working. Despite every indication from her that he was unwelcome, he still ached for her in

every bone of his body. She clearly had no idea how rav-
ishing she looked in that revealing T-shirt and those tight
jeans. He didn't know how he'd stopped himself from cup-
ping his hands around that neat rear, though somehow he'd
managed. Nevertheless, he'd not been able to prevent himself from flirting! What the hell was he doing?

He shouldn't be touching her, but she was like a drug
and he couldn't stop himself from craving more and more
of her. Frustration was making him worse. He couldn't resist any opportunity to be near her. God knew what his
eyes were telling her. It wouldn't surprise him if he were
arrested for mentally salacious assault.

She made him conscious of the good things in life. Like
laughter. He grinned. Even her put-downs made him laugh!

As he watched her, she became more frantic, the lovely
curving lines of her back becoming stiff and rigid. He had
two choices: to take her in his arms, kiss her passionately
and resolve this desperate wanting, or leave her alone.

He knew what he longed to do. Such an action would
inevitably provoke a sharp rebuke from her. Maybe a slap.
A piece of her mind. Then he'd have no option but to
apologise and leave. It would be over.

Yet it would be a dishonourable move to make. After
all, he wasn't a callow youth, casting away rational thought
in order to satisfy an unconquerable desire. Even if he felt
like one, dammit! No, he should earn his rejection some
other way. A straightforward insulting suggestion, perhaps.
He had to remember that she belonged to someone else.
The faithful Tim.

The objection was noted. He knew immediately that he
intended to ignore it. He moved towards her. She turned,
her eyes wide with alarm. Then he was looking down on
her, frowning because her body seemed to be softening,
and her expression had become suddenly voluptuous and
sensual.

He didn't stop to ask himself why. Slowly his gaze
drifted over the parts his mouth would ravage. Her lips
were parted, ready for him. He drew in a sharp, ragged

breath and her long black lashes flickered down to her cheeks, almost as if in submission.

Hazily he angled his head, prolonging the delicious moment between spine-tingling anticipation and the actual, heart-stopping reality of the kiss.

CHAPTER THREE

'WHAT are you doing, you wicked man? Leave her alone, you—you gangster!'

Both Adam and Trish leapt apart at the grating cry of outrage from the cottage behind them. Startled, Trish tripped on the handle of the hoe and fell against Adam. His arms automatically came around her, twisting her round, bringing them both heavily to the ground.

Then Trish felt heavy blows raining down on Adam's unprotected body and she tried instinctively to shield him. While he covered his head in a brief, involuntary movement, she looked up, just as Adam rolled over, grabbed the stout stick and wrenched it away.

'*Gran!*' yelled Trish in astonishment. 'Stop! It's OK!'

She began to laugh. Adam did too. The sight of a little white-haired old lady trying to beat the daylights out of an immensely powerful male was too funny for words.

'He was creeping up on you!' Gran said defiantly. 'You didn't know he was there and then you turned—'

'Oh, I knew he was there,' Trish muttered, well aware that she'd been hoping, willing him to take her in his arms and kiss the breath from her body.

'Here.' Adam had got to his feet and was looking oddly at her. 'Thanks for shielding me.' He held out his hand.

Wisely she dispensed with his help and managed on her own. 'This is so embarrassing! Are you all right?' she asked him in concern.

'His trousers aren't,' Gran said with malicious satisfaction.

Trish's gaze went to Adam's slim hips. The beige trousers were streaked with grass stains. He brushed leaves from his thighs, briefly stretching the material over taut

55

muscles. She swallowed and dragged her gaze away, aware
that it had lingered a little too long.

'I'm sorry,' she said breathily. 'You'd do better to wear
something tough and hard-wearing here, like jeans—'

'Why? Is this a daily performance?' Adam asked, his
eyes brimming with wry humour.

Trish giggled. 'Who can tell? Gran's a bit unpredictable,'
she whispered under her breath. 'Dear Gran!' she went on
affectionately. 'This is Adam Foster. Petra's stepfather.
Adam, my grandmother, Mrs Hicks.' They shook hands
warily. 'You remember I went to stay with the family in
Truro?' she reminded her grandmother.

'Do I! You came back unexpected in a terrible fret. Some
man at the bottom of that, I thought.'

Trish went pink. One of the few occasions when her
grandmother's memory worked perfectly, and it had to be
this one!

'Adam's staying for a week or so—'

'Oh! I get it! Say no more. You've got together again.
He was creeping up to snatch a quick kiss!'

'No!' They both shouted in unison. They looked at one
another in alarm.

Patting Trish's arm, her grandmother gave a knowing
grin and tapped the side of her nose. 'I'll keep quiet. Better
you,' she said to the stunned Adam, 'than that Tony.'

'Tim,' Trish said patiently, for what seemed like the mil-
lionth time.

'Nice boy,' her grandmother conceded. 'Got no fire,
though. Ted isn't the kind of—'

'Tim!' insisted Trish.

'Whoever.' Her grandmother gave a dismissive wave of
her hand. 'Trish needs a real man, like you, with a bit of
life in him.'

'Thanks,' murmured Adam, hugely entertained.

'Yes,' Gran said, assessing him critically. 'I think you'll
do nicely—'

'Gran!' protested Trish, abashed and amused in equal

measures. 'You can't say things like that! You make me want to run away and hide!'

'You wouldn't.' Gran recovered her stick. 'You'd be fretting about me, wondering if I was all right.' She turned to Adam. 'Very caring girl, is Trish. She looked after her mother for a year, rather than see her die in some foreign nursing home on St Mary's. She'll make sure I pop my clogs within sight of Seal Rock. Got a tender heart, Trish has. You couldn't do better.'

'I'm sure you're right,' Adam said quietly, humouring her.

'Don't encourage her!' complained Trish, infuriated at being the butt of the joke. 'He's not interested in me, Gran!' she added firmly.

'Course he is! Look at your faces! You, beetroot-red; him, all smug and self-satisfied.'

Trish and Adam stole covert glances at one another, their expressions becoming instantly unreadable.

'Nonsense! I've been scrabbling on the ground and Adam's merely relieved to be alive! You're embarrassing me, Gran—as usual!' She turned to Adam, knowing she could only joke her way out of this one. 'I'm waiting for Gran to pair me up with that wealthy shipowner who's been in the news. She said he had good prospects, the other day.'

'He has.' Adam's innocent expression turned to laughter again. 'Don't worry,' he said reassuringly. 'I won't expect you to honour any proposals of marriage your grandmother makes on your behalf.'

A pain sawed jaggedly through her breast and she caught at it with her hand, placing her palm against her heart to contain her bitterness.

'There,' she said unsteadily, putting her arm around her grandmother's bony shoulders. 'Got the message? He wasn't trying to kiss me—'

'Oh, yes, he was. Saw him about to grab you, didn't I?'

Trish raised her eyes to the heavens. 'I should have warned you, Adam,' she sighed. 'Gran is very forthright.'

'I don't mind. I rather like it,' he said drily. 'Can I walk you back to the cottage, Mrs Hicks?' he suggested, a gleam in his eyes.

'Nice manners,' Gran approved. 'But I'm not incapable of finding my own front door after eighty-five years. I'm not senile, you know.' She set off to her cottage and, with a voice loud enough to reach right across the island, called, 'You stay and give her a decent kiss and cuddle!'

'He'll do nothing of the sort!' cried Trish, feeling horribly hot and bothered. 'Any more of this and I'll ring the men in white coats to take you away!'

'They'd have a job,' murmured Adam.

Despite her embarrassment, Trish grinned. 'I think you're right. Gran!' she called. 'I'm going in to get dinner ready. You two can do what you like.'

'Let him help,' called her grandmother over her shoulder.

'Lucy's coming. I don't need help!' Trish yelled back.

Her grandmother paused by the honeysuckle bower. 'If he's your only guest, what do you need with Lucy? You'll never make any money that way!'

'I don't need her,' sighed Trish, heading for the kitchen door. 'Lucy needs me.'

'We all do. Him as well, by the looks of him!'

With her grandmother's knowing cackle in her rapidly reddening ears, Trish went into the house and put on an apron.

Adam exchanged smiles with the strangely silent Lucy, picked up Mrs Hicks's escapee wool for the fifth time and tucked it in her knitting basket.

'I think you're a fraud,' he said calmly to the old lady. 'You see more than you let on.'

'Trish doesn't know what she's missing,' declared Mrs Hicks. 'Tell her I'm staying over with my friend in town tonight and shut the door on your way out.'

Knowing when he was being dismissed, he bade his goodbyes, restraining a grin at the thought of the ten or so houses by Bryher quay being dignified with the title of 'town'.

An excitement gripped him as he walked towards Trish's cottage. Once Trish's grandmother had told him that Trish felt deeply about him, that she had never stood *that* close to Tim in normal conversation, and her eyes didn't dilate so obviously, he'd been overwhelmed by what he'd wanted to do to Trish. Touch her, kiss her, make love to her, make her cry out in pleasure...

He checked himself. This was taking him over. He'd built his reputation by being strong-minded, tough and decisive. With Trish, he felt anything but.

Why was he risking his emotions by hankering after her? Why did he care that she was wasting herself on Tim, Tom, Tony? The old woman had made it plain that she didn't think the young shop assistant was worthy of Trish. He tended to agree. The odd picnic and trip to the cinema didn't make for a vibrant relationship. The passion was, according to Mrs Hicks, totally absent.

So, despite all the warnings in his head, he was hell-bent on finding out if the old woman was right. A potentially fatal combination of vanity and curiosity! But he had to discover the truth.

He twisted the ring on his finger. Soon he'd know, one way or the other.

By the time Adam wandered in, Trish's blood pressure had climbed down from its dangerous level and her heart had stopped sending tom-tom messages to distant Africa.

Adam was sensible. He'd make allowances for Gran. And, being the gentleman he was, he'd pretend he didn't know that many of Gran's claims were deadly accurate.

'Been for a walk?' she asked conversationally.

'Talking to your grandmother.'

'Oh, crumbs.'

She shot him a cautious look. He leant against the pine dresser with the simmering excitement of a man who'd just won the lottery. She blinked and hastily avoided his eyes. They were bright and full of fire, piercing into hers with an unnerving intensity. It was very unsettling, she thought in agitation, having a drop-dead gorgeous man hanging around.

'She's fascinating,' he observed. 'Riveting, in fact.'

Out of the corner of her eye she saw him fold his arms decisively. Something had happened. Nervously she turned on the blender, disconcerted by the energy pouring from him and the off-putting air of intent.

'You're being very kind to Gran, considering she tried to beat the daylights out of you,' she managed, shouting over the machine.

He smiled with sinister charm. 'She wanted me to open a jar for her.'

Trish frowned. 'She's got a device.'

'I know. I recommended one. She said she'd lost it.'

Damn! She'd over-blended the soup! Crossly, she flung in some more leek and parsnip chunks, flicked on the switch for a few moments and then sprinkled in some fresh coriander leaves.

'That was an excuse. I saw the opener,' she told him curtly. 'When I washed up for her.'

He shrugged carelessly. 'No matter. We had an interesting chat.'

Help! As casually as possible, she asked, 'What about?'

There was a moment's pause. 'Knitting.'

'You were riveted by her *knitting*?' she asked incredulously.

'It is rather...er...unique. She told me how she was always dropping stitches and you never showed your impatience with her, but unfailingly set her straight again.'

'Sorry,' Trish said, mortified by her grandmother's matchmaking. 'I'm afraid she's trying to promote me into your good books.'

'Successfully. I'm convinced you're devoted,' he said solemnly, either deliberately misunderstanding her remark or courteously choosing to do so. 'Extraordinary, her knitting. She's very proud of it, isn't she?' He was having difficulty keeping a straight face. 'Interesting...er...scarf. If that's what it is?'

Trish caught his eye and laughed, sharing the joke. 'Could be an overland bridge to Tresco when it's finished, for all I know! We measured it the other day. It's nine feet four inches long! She drops stitches on an average of three times a day. I've perfected the art of sorting them out in between all my other jobs. She likes to keep her hands as mobile as possible for as long as possible, you see.'

'You're very good to her,' he said softly.

'It's mutual. She looked after me when Mum died.'

'I thought you were the one who did the looking after?'

'I wasn't talking about doing jobs like shopping and cooking. I meant emotionally.'

His eyes darkened. 'I see. You were lucky to have her,' he said, sounding strangely withdrawn.

Trish's hands, busily crumbling the Stilton, suddenly stilled. 'We all need a shoulder to lean on sometimes,' she said gently, realising why he was looking so strained. She decided to come out in the open about the mistake she'd made. 'We both needed comforting, didn't we, when Christine died?'

'I don't go in for self-pity. Or dwelling on the past.'

His tone and whole demeanour told her to keep off. He saw his ruthless elimination of anything that might touch his emotions as being a strength. She wasn't sure.

He'd always been uptight about certain things that had caught her heartstrings. Like that disabled child her catering college had subsidised, so that the kiddie could go to America for special treatment. Adam had cut her off in mid-explanation, written a huge cheque and told her not to discuss it again.

It was his choice to keep his emotions under wraps. Nothing to do with her. She saw the tightness of his expression and sought to relax him, knowing that she did so because she cared too much.

'You've been decent about Gran's brutality,' she said jokingly. 'Anywhere else, she might be locked up. Here, her funny ways are tolerated. I usually prime guests about her,' she explained, smiling up at him. 'She says what she thinks and that can be disconcerting! And she's always getting the wrong end of the stick.'

He rubbed his shoulder. 'Are you kidding? I'd say she'd got the right end of the stick!'

As she giggled, Trish's sharp eyes noticed him wince. She wiped her hands on her apron. 'Do you…?' She hesitated. 'If you think you're developing bruises, perhaps I ought to treat them…'

Heavy black lashes hid his eyes, his attention apparently caught by the bunch of wild garlic on the dresser. Touching the dainty white blooms with a surprisingly delicate touch, he said, 'I think I'm stiffening up.' He looked up suddenly, his expression unreadable. 'What do you think?'

'I could…rub something in that would help,' she offered, her concern getting the better of her wariness.

'Uh-uh.' He gave that some thought. 'Yes. OK. Might be a good idea.'

Adam began to unbutton his shirt. Slowly. As if concentrating hard. She found that she was holding her breath. Annoyed with her stupidity, she became brisk and efficient, reaching down the first-aid box and removing the bottle of flower water. There was a whisper of cotton as the shirt was dropped to a chair.

'Let's hope your grandmother doesn't come in,' Adam murmured wickedly. 'She'd get entirely the wrong idea. I'd be thrashed all over again!'

Trish gave a quick roll of her eyes. 'She's a tiger!' Surprised by the husky croak which had emerged, she swallowed hard and reluctantly, longingly, raised her eyes to his naked chest.

He hooked a hand under the chair and carried it to the back door, tilting it so that it was wedged under the door handle. 'Precautions,' he said smoothly into the hushed silence.

Of course it was a sensible move. Anyone could wander in and get the wrong impression. But something about his movements—or her thoughts, perhaps—made this seem to be a preparation for an illicit act. A tremor of fear and inexplicable excitement trickled through Trish as Adam moved purposefully towards her.

'Where does it feel…uncomfortable?' she asked, making an only adequate attempt to sound offhand.

'Mainly across my back.'

'Turn around.'

Her voice had become just a whisper. For several moments, Adam didn't react—probably because he was startled by her huskiness. Knowing he'd be frowning at her helpless infatuation, she dared not meet his eyes. Instead, she remained frozen, staring at the magnificent spread of his chest. Toned. Tanned…

A tan. Skiing? The Caribbean? She remembered Louise's echoing remarks and flashed her anguished eyes up to his. 'Turn,' she snapped out curtly, and he turned with a tightening of his mouth. His fiancée was now firmly in her mind.

There were some faint marks across his shoulders and she dabbed the diluted arnica on them perfunctorily. Every muscle seemed to be under tension. A surge of sympathy overcame her qualms and she took her time, making sure she covered the area carefully. She also worked slowly because it was a delight to touch his back, to stroke him and watch the ripples of muscle playing beneath the velvety skin.

'Takes a long while, doesn't it?' he commented in a low, honeyed drawl.

She flushed. Had it?

'You have to do it properly,' she said defensively. 'I've finished now. The stiffness should ease off. Gran's never done anything like this before. I really am sorry,' she added humbly.

'Thanks.' He didn't put his shirt on, but leaned comfortably against the dresser again, watching Trish while she washed her hands and began hulling strawberries. 'I won't sue her,' he teased. 'She was defending you. God knows who she thought I was!'

'Jack the Ripper, I think.' Trish flashed him a wry grin. 'Or Casanova.'

'Formidable lady. I think she'd challenge stampeding elephants if you were threatened.'

Trish beamed. 'I'd do the same for her. She's a darling. I love her very much. She can be a bit wacky at times—'

'I know!' he said with a laugh.

'No, I mean as in crazy!' She was laughing with him, thinking how like old times this was. 'Sometimes she forgets things—like eating. Sometimes she's as sharp as a knife. You never can tell. It makes each day chancy—but exciting!' Agitated by the warmth of his eyes, she checked her watch. 'That's odd! Lucy should be here by now.'

'She's not coming,' he announced casually.

Trish's eyes opened wide in astonishment. 'What do you mean?'

'Your grandmother waylaid her as I was leaving.'

And wider. 'What for?'

'Company,' he said glibly. 'Oh. And your grandmother's staying overnight with a friend. Why does Lucy need you?'

Trish felt totally disorientated. Gran was behaving in a most peculiar fashion. Lucy, too. And Adam... Why was he looking at her in that serious, affectionate way? Was her hair decorated with blobs of Stilton? Somehow she dragged her mind back to his question. But she couldn't take her eyes from the satin skin stretched over his collar-bone and the heavy pulse in the vulnerable little hollow at the base of his throat.

'Lucy,' she said with the slow, deliberate air of an alcoholic trying to pretend she was sober, 'is another person I have to warn you about.'

'Sounds like a story coming up. Life here,' he murmured, thrusting his hands into his pockets and looking devastatingly nonchalant and at ease, 'is absolutely fascinating. Tell me about the gorgeous Lucy's particular peculiarities.'

Absorbed in the movement of his mouth, she was unaware that her lashes had fluttered and her huge eyes had become deep, sapphire pools of longing. Adam drew in a huge breath, lifting his torso so that it was taut and gleaming in the late evening sun.

'She…' Trish tried again, struck by the irony of her confused speech. 'She stutters.'

The smile was wiped from his face and a bleakness replaced it. Several seconds elapsed before he seemed capable of speaking himself, and by then his expression had become shuttered. Trish watched him very closely, knowing that something in his past was hurting him, and wishing she could talk to him about it.

'That's why she said nothing! I wondered… Poor girl,' he said at last. He hesitated, on the brink of telling her something, then said, 'I know what that's like. It's hell. People treat you like an idiot.' He met her look of surprise with his steady gaze, his expression still unreadable. 'I'm a recovering stammerer,' he said in a low tone.

'*You!*' Trish cried in amazement.

'Me.'

And suddenly she realised she knew nothing about him—and wanted to hear it all: his childhood, his teenage years, where he went to school, how he got his first job…

But all that was Louise's prerogative, she told herself. Intimate little chats over the computer keyboards during a coffee break. In bed. After sex. She began to scrape the new potatoes as if she had no further interest in him.

'I'd never have guessed in a million years,' she said, annoyed that she sounded as if she were making cocktail-party chatter: bright, cheerful, her voice pitched somewhere near the ceiling.

'I control it by breathing,' he offered after a moment. 'It's a method that works with some people, but not everyone. You want to know more?'

Yes. Everything, she thought passionately. Especially *why* someone as confident and assured as Adam had ever suffered from a speech impediment. But she'd betray herself—especially the fact that she could feel his pain.

'Not really,' she replied, hoping she sounded vaguely bored. 'I'd like Lucy to try this breathing technique, though.'

'I'd be delighted to teach her—' he began earnestly.

'No!' cried Trish, anxious to protect the shy young girl. 'She'd never let you! She's terribly self-conscious. Don't upset her—'

'Whatever you say!' He held up his hands in a gesture of surrender. 'I wouldn't hurt her for the world.'

'You won't draw attention to it if she tries to speak, will you?' she asked, worrying that he'd make Lucy worse.

'Please! I know what it's like better than most. I'm not entirely insensitive, Trish.'

The gentle rebuke made her feel ashamed of her lack of trust. 'Sorry! Forgive me, Adam! I'm so used to protecting her from people. I know you've got a kind heart.'

There was an imperceptible twist to his mouth. 'Not as generous as yours. You're one of life's carers. You employ Lucy, even when you don't need her...'

'Wouldn't you?' she asked in surprise. 'Wouldn't any-one?'

'Not necessarily. Most people act for their own selfish reasons.'

'Not here, they don't. We look after each other. Lucy needs a boost to her self-confidence. She needs to meet people. I'm teaching her how to cook. I want her to go on the same course I did,' she said fervently, trying to avoid Adam's sultry, brooding gaze. 'She'll have a sense of pur-pose then, a feeling of achievement. Why don't you put your shirt on?' she finished irritably. Having Adam around was bad enough, but a half-nude Adam was testing her to the limit!

'Not much point. I'll go and have a shower in a moment,' he answered with a lazy smile.

'Stay there much longer and I'll give you a job,' she threatened.

'Fine by me. I don't know anything about cooking, though.' He eyed the potatoes as though they were hand grenades.

'Time you learnt,' she muttered grimly. 'There are things every husband-to-be should know.'

Though for the life of her she couldn't picture Adam and

Louise doing domestic chores together. They'd have servants, of course. What was the fun in that?

Adam, however, had apparently been galvanised by the thought of learning a spouse's job. He'd moved to her side in a flash, washed his hands, and was now nudging her hip with his.

'Move over!' he complained cheerfully, eager to begin his husbandly chores.

Trish felt like sulking at his enthusiasm. Here she was, side by side with the most hunky guy in the Northern Hemisphere, and she was teaching him the art of being a New Man—someone else's! Scraping potatoes, of all things! Just her luck. Other women would have chosen something glamorous or sexy, like 'Wining and Dining', or 'Bedside Approaches', she thought crossly, handing him a knife. But, no, she had to be up to her armpits in peelings over a kitchen sink!

She sucked in a huge breath of resignation. Adam's whole body tensed as he began to attack the potato in his hand. Seeing there'd be nothing left unless she intervened, she put her hand quickly over his.

His eyes flashed dangerously in response and Trish drew her hand away, quickly, too shocked by the instantly sexual images which had come into her head to wonder why.

She and Adam. Naked, exploring each other inch by inch. The curve of his neat buttocks, the thrust of his powerful thighs...

'Yes?' he enquired in an undertone, jerking her out of her paralysis.

Yes, please. She needed him. Her whole body was aching, tuned into every move he made, preoccupied with satisfying her insatiable lust.

Horrified by the baseness of her instincts, she stared at the scraps of peel, trying to remember what she'd been doing.

'I forget... No! I remember!' she cried in relief. 'Leave some of the white stuff,' she said, forcing an exasperated

tone and pointing to the sad remnant of potato in his hand.
'That's the part we're going to eat, idiot!'

'Right. I lost concentration,' he admitted, with a slow,
heart-warming smile.

Trish put on a schoolmarm frown. She wasn't having
him dreaming of Louise while she was around! 'Well,
don't,' she said sharply. 'Watch more closely.'

He did, taking her instruction literally. Welded to her
side, he bent his head to hers; she was tensely aware of his
lashes brushing his cheeks and the solemn set of his mouth.
She was conscious, too, of the warm, male smell of him,
the terrible proximity of his naked chest and the fact that
his bare arms were brushing hers. Beautiful arms. Shapely,
with a light covering of fine, dark hairs whose silkiness was
sending shivers of eroticism up and down her spine.

'You're an extraordinary person, Trish,' he said, so softly
that she found herself straining towards him to make out
his muttered comment.

'I know.' Her mouth settled into an uncharacteristic pout.
Stupid enough, unfair enough, to want someone else's man.
Disconsolately she scraped away. 'Gran says I'm peculiar
too.'

'I said *extra ordinary*.'

The words vibrated with a strange richness. Perhaps because they had been pitched lower than usual, they sounded
unusually heartfelt. Trish was just telling herself that she'd
obviously started fantasising and was well on her way to
fairyland when he reached across her to drop his finished
potato into the saucepan on the draining-board. He took an
unbearably long time about it—so long that it seemed he
was issuing an open invitation.

More than willing to accept, she almost leaned forward
and kissed the infinitely desirable line of his jaw. Before
she did, he had straightened, dropped the knife, fished it
out of the bowl of water and dropped it again. He looked
at it with helpless exasperation, then grasped it decisively.

Trish struggled to keep the atmosphere friendly and to

make amends for the way she'd misinterpreted his body language.

'Why do you say that about me?' she asked curiously.

He was having some difficulty co-ordinating his movements. 'What?'

She grinned. The ultra-efficient Adam was well out of his element! 'Me. Not ordinary.'

'Because you take on responsibilities that others would shirk. You can't have been very old when you looked after your mother. Didn't you say once that she'd died when you were fifteen? How did you manage with schoolwork?'

'Fairly well.' She grimaced. 'I suppose I failed more exams than I might have done. Gran was more active then—the arthritis hadn't got to her,' Trish explained, glad they were talking about normal things. 'She ran the guest-house business and looked after Mum during the week. I went to the secondary school on St Mary's, you see.'

'A long way to travel every day.'

He was listening very intently, as if he was interested in the small details of her life. Flattered, she felt encouraged to tell him more.

'But I didn't. That would be a nightmare! Especially in the winter gales! Bryher children go to Tresco school from the age of five to eleven. Then, like all children from the out islands, they stay on St Mary's from Monday to Friday. For the year she was ill, I looked after Mum on the weekends and holidays, did the week's shopping, cooked great batches of stuff for the week ahead—pies, stews, puddings and so on. I cleaned the cottage and did the washing and ironing, so that Gran wouldn't have too much to do.'

'I had no idea. You didn't tell me.'

'Christine took all our spare time, didn't she?' Trish reminded him. 'We were too busy to delve into the whole of my past. And nursing my mother who was dying of cancer wasn't the kind of thing I could chat about to Christine.'

'We asked a lot of you. And you gave it,' he commented thoughtfully. 'You helped to care for your mother, then my wife, and now your grandmother. Don't you ever want time to yourself? To be free?'

Trish laughed. 'I *am* free! I'm doing what I love!' A gentle smile spread over her face, lighting her eyes with warmth and affection. 'If people you care for are in need, you give of yourself without feeling any sense of hardship.'

He seemed to be struggling to understand that. 'You must have grown up rather faster than most,' he observed.

'I suppose so. We're all used to turning our hands to anything and everything that needs doing. We pull together. We're a real old-fashioned community. It's hard work but lots of fun. The cottage was always full of laughter when Mum was there,' she recalled fondly. 'Bryher people used to pop in and tell her what they'd been doing and sometimes she'd be surrounded by a dozen people, telling tall and utterly improbable tales!'

'Now I understand why you were so skilled at handling the people in the hospice,' said Adam, his mouth soft with smiles as she recounted the happy memories. 'You don't see imminent death as a reason to tiptoe around and look glum.'

'It depends. You don't want someone being bright and breezy if you feel dire,' she said quietly, throwing a handful of mint leaves into the saucepan. Both she and Adam leaned forward to sniff the aroma and bumped into one another in the process. 'Sorry!' she mumbled, her eyes huge with alarm.

'I'm not!'

His hand caught her chin and turned her face to his, cradling it with a firm intent that weakened her legs instantly. Her huge eyes searched his in wonder.

'What are you doing?' she gasped in panic.

'What I was going to do before your grandmother appeared. Relax,' he soothed. 'It had to be.'

She couldn't speak. Desire drugged his eyes: desire for her. Bewildered, she let her lashes flutter down, her gaze fixed on the wickedly carnal lines of his mouth. She felt overwhelmed by his sex appeal. Deliciously defenceless.

'No!' she whispered, denying herself. And then, knowing how close she was to capitulating, she cried more vehemently, a note of desperation in her voice, 'No! Leave me alone, Adam!'

Instantly he moved back, apparently not at all put out that she had rejected his pass. She had the distinct impression that his intention had been postponed, not abandoned. Nervously, she picked up a bowl of herbs and then put it down again because her hands were shaking so much. This was awful. They were both acting badly...

He *knew* she wanted him. She was obviously sending out signals to him and that was why he'd tried to kiss her, believing she was encouraging him. He was a man, after all, and weren't men by their very nature easily aroused? She'd stalled him for now. But he had only to exert a little more pressure on her and she'd find him impossible to resist.

He's engaged, she told herself tersely. Off limits.

'I think I'll unpack, shower and make a few calls before dinner,' he announced calmly. A small, wry smile lifted the corners of his mouth. 'I suppose we don't need the barricade now, do we?'

Confused and shamed by the implication that she'd connived in his plan to steal forbidden kisses, she made no reply. Lowering her head, she mechanically arranged the chops on the grill pan. In a moment or two he had grown bored with her silence and had replaced the chair, picked up his shirt and left the room.

She cooked the meal. Ignored him when he came down at seven-fifteen for a drink. Served the first course, then the second, and all the while they remained tense and silent. The sexual tension in the room was unbearable. It was like walking into an electric storm.

'You...didn't like this?' she asked anxiously, seeing his soup was barely touched.

'What? Sorry, Trish. I was miles away. No, it was excellent. I'm a bit preoccupied. Problems at work.' He fiddled with the stem of his wineglass. 'I have to return to London tomorrow.'

A silence fell. She stared at him, dismayed by the strength of her disappointment. 'Permanently?' she asked unhappily.

His lashes flicked up as if to check her expression. She drew in a sharp breath, knowing well what his eyes were telling her. *This could be the only chance we have of being together. Take it or leave it.*

'Difficult to say.'

Feeling like bursting into tears, she carried the plates out and absently slid them into the sink. He was leaving— maybe never to return. Her reaction appalled her.

She wanted him. Desired him so much that she didn't know what to do with herself, other than to hide her feelings as much as possible. Carefully, she placed the dishes for the main course on a tray, took a deep breath and carried everything in. Adam was thoughtfully sipping wine, his expression taut with concentration. When he looked up at her, it was as if his dark eyes were intent on seeing right into her head.

Without speaking, she slid the plate in front of him, painfully conscious of how close she was to him. He was clearly hot and had taken off his sage linen jacket to reveal an expensive cream shirt which matched exactly his cream chinos. Unable to avoid thinking of his body beneath, she gave a little shudder as goose-pimples crawled up her spine. Hurriedly, she left the room.

After a decent interval and three furtive glasses of fortifying wine, she returned with the strawberries.

'Trish... My apologies. I couldn't do justice to your cooking, delicious though it was.' He paused, his long, slim fingers following the curves of a serving spoon.

'Work,' she supposed, swallowing nervously.

'No.'

He wasn't looking at her but she knew he was as wound up as she was. Her breathing became shallow when she began to collect the dishes. Something was drawing her to him and she stood far too close for one brief, unwise second. It was long enough.

In that time, Adam's eyes had locked with hers, one hand had caught her outstretched arm and the other had splayed on the small of her back, pulling her against his thigh.

'You. You've ruined...*one* appetite of mine,' he said in soft reproach.

'I'm...sorry!' she answered stupidly, her throat dry from the implication.

Visibly simmering with a frightening, pent-up sexual energy, he swung around in his chair, his legs trapping hers. The pressure of his fingers pressing on her firm rear jerked her forwards till she could feel the heat between his thighs.

'We have to settle this, Trish!'

She stared down at him, completely transfixed by his compelling eyes. 'Settle...what?' she asked warily, but gulped, knowing what he meant. She had to stop luring him with unguarded, longing glances. Maybe she couldn't help herself, but it wasn't fair—

Adam rose in a sudden movement which knocked over the chair. Both of them ignored it and Trish felt her heart stop, then pound heavily at the determination in his expression. Dismayed, she could only gaze hungrily at him, unable to conceal how badly she wanted to be kissed.

'You and me,' he said.

Somehow she shook her head in denial and attempted to pull away. He held her fast.

'There is no you and me,' she lied painfully. Her body language, however, told the real truth.

'There is.' His eyes gleamed beneath hooded lids. 'I wish there weren't but...we can't ignore it.'

Ignoring her little whimper of protest, he drew her more securely into his arms. She trembled, betraying how close she was to surrender.

'Adam...' she mumbled in dismay.

'I want you!' he muttered fiercely, almost despairingly.

She felt herself melt into him. With a low growl in his throat that created primitive curls of anticipation throughout

her whole body, he slowly, tantalisingly, lowered his mouth
to hers. Their lips were almost touching. But not quite. She
stood there helplessly, all her nerves knotted and expectant,
her mouth tingling as she waited in the breathless silence.

Through hazy eyes, she watched his lips become fuller,
the sensual arches more strongly carved. And she knew that
she was responding in the same way, her teeth gleaming
like his, her shortened breath mingling with his, sharp and
hard.

Just as she thought she'd die of waiting, his mouth
touched hers with an incredible gentleness. A groan and a
shudder ran through him. And suddenly he was kissing her
with a ferocity which she welcomed because she could
press fiercely against him and release some of the suppressed hunger at last.

She closed her eyes ecstatically, slipping her hands up to
cradle his face, touching the smooth forehead. Drifting her
fingers over his angled brows, she slid her palms to the
strong neck.

Wonderful…all she'd ever dreamed of. Her love for him,
the madness that possessed her, erased everything from her
mind and left only an uncontainable joy which filled her
whole being and made her body surge with happiness.

Oblivious to everything but his kisses, she drowned in
the delight of his searching mouth. His need excited her;
she could hear it in the harshness of his breath, feel it in
the frenzy of impatience as he clutched at her and subdued
any likely protests with his hard, possessive kisses.

For a moment he drew back, staring at her with a yearning, dizzying gaze, and then his mouth returned to hers,
kissing it tenderly, over and over again, till it felt warm
and swollen and she was desperate for him to go further.

His hand must have slipped beneath her shirt, because
she felt his touch on the bare flesh of her high breast and
heard his feral growl when he realised she wore nothing
beneath. After a second or two of tense and vibrating silence, he gripped the edges of the fabric and wrenched the

buttons free, exposing her nakedness. She waited in agony for their flesh to touch.

He was still. Somehow she made her heavy-lidded eyes open and saw that he was studying every inch of her: the soft curve of her shoulders, the hollow at the base of her throat, her throbbing, ripe breasts, already hard and engorged from wanting his touch for so long.

His hands dropped away. His body was trembling as if it was under great stress. He didn't touch her breasts as she expected, but leaned towards her so that only their lips touched. In that tantalising position, he teased her mouth till it parted. Even then, he held himself back, infuriating her, driving her crazy, her breathing becoming shorter with every languorous sweep of the tip of his tongue along the inside of her lips.

All the muscles in her body had turned to a flowing liquid. She could hardly bear the suspense and hated him for his extraordinary self-control. Blindly, she reached out for his waist, but he pushed her hands away, leaving her moaning in frustration.

And then...and then... A shudder rocked through them both. His mouth was still covering hers, his tongue flicking now in and out between her lips, but he had imperceptibly touched the deep swell of each breast with his fingertips, brushing over the welling curves, and she was gasping, groaning, demanding...

'I want you!' she whispered helplessly.

Softly, sweetly, his mouth enclosed each desperate nipple, suckling with such a deep delight that shook her profoundly. Somehow they were moving from the room but the intensity of Adam's assault didn't lessen. Vaguely she was aware that they were in the hall, and then he had swept her up in his arms, raining passionate kisses on her face and throat as he stumbled up the stairs.

'Trish, oh, Trish!' he murmured urgently into her mouth.

His desperation made her feel all-powerful and totally desirable. Abandoning herself to the moment, she took his face in her hands and kissed him deeply, feeling herself being lowered as she did so, and the softness of a duvet beneath her.

The whole length of his body covered hers, his weight a joy so welcome and overpoweringly erotic that she emitted breathy little gasps of pleasure. As Adam frantically fought to remove his shirt, her body arched in demand, her pelvis strained to his, unknowingly inviting him to make love to her totally.

He resisted her, preferring to delay, to tease and tantalise. Knowing this, aware he was finding it hard to control his hunger, she took the initiative. She didn't want to wait. She wanted him *now*. She ran her hands over his naked torso and then impatiently fumbled with his belt, breathing out angry whimpers of fury when it refused to unclip. His hand covered hers, preventing it from continuing.

Raging with passion, she flashed him a look of imperious demand. And then she was crushed to him, her mouth bruised with savage kisses, her body hard against his again, flesh to flesh, feeling his need, frightened and thrilled by it.

She loved him, she thought hazily, returning his kisses with a wild elation, and she knew that she had always loved him.

'Make love to me!' she whispered, her eyes bright with fevered adoration.

Adam's eyes blazed into hers and in her heightened state she imagined they were full of pained love. She clung to him, captured by her own heart, while he kissed and touched her, skilfully removing items of clothing till they were both naked.

The feel of his body, strong, demanding and utterly virile, made her feel wonderfully feminine and alluring. She was more than ready for him, her body pliant and supple, open and welcoming.

'I need you, Trish! I need you so badly!' he gasped.

'And I need you!' Eagerly she guided him, bucking when he entered her, shuddering in shock, but her hands urged him on. 'Yes, Adam! Oh, please... Yes...harder...faster, *more*!' she implored.

Something took over her body—she wasn't fully conscious of what she did, only that she was making love with the man she had always adored. Incredible elation filled every inch of her, a wild and unstoppable physical energy gripped her and she welcomed the fierceness of their loving, needing its roughness, slaking her thirst for his lips and satisfying the long-denied aridity of her body.

I love him! she exulted, aware of nothing but sensation, every particle of her absorbed by Adam...her lover. And then they were both overcome by raw, primal responses as their bodies climbed to a shattering mutual climax which left them both slicked in sweat and incapable of moving or speaking.

They floated into a deep silence which was broken only by their regular, laboured breathing. Trish lay in a state of total bliss, every muscle loose and relaxed. Sleepily she was aware that Adam was tucking her up in the bed. Other than a smug smile of satisfaction, her only reaction was to hold out her arms to him, and she fell asleep almost instantly, cuddled up in his protective embrace.

CHAPTER FOUR

THE dawn chorus shot Trish into a brutal awareness. For a brief moment she lay snuggled in the curve of Adam's naked body, his arm flung possessively across her, his hand resting on the swell of her hip.

And then a coldness stole through her, chilling her to the bone. *What had she done?*

She grew rigid with horror. Adam loved someone else. Louise had been betrayed by them both. Trish's eyes widened in utter dismay. She'd made a mockery of everything she believed in: fidelity, honesty, consideration for others…

Suddenly she felt sick with shame. A shaft of light gleamed on Adam's gold signet ring and it flashed accusingly at her. She had to get away! The thought of Adam waking, turning to her with a smile and caressing her, coaxing her to make love again, just filled her with horror.

Gingerly, she inched herself away from him, her heart in her mouth when he murmured her name and sighed in his sleep. Her alarmed eyes slanted to his face, her mouth trembling at his ecstatic smile and rumpled hair. Fiercely, she suppressed the quickening feelings of affection and forced herself to slide out of bed, tiptoeing to the bathroom.

Shaking with misery, she turned the shower on and stepped into it. First scalding hot, then icy cold. He'd wanted her; she'd obliged. How tacky, cheap, nasty…!

She'd made a fool of herself. Last night had meant nothing to Adam—it had only been a bit of fun as far as he was concerned. Perhaps this was the first time for a while that he'd been parted from Louise and his sex drive had overcome his common sense. He'd be appalled too, she thought, wondering how they'd handle the situation. It would be so awkward and she felt dreadful.

And now her feelings for him were even deeper than

before. Adam was the man she wanted. But he'd fallen for
the beautiful Louise. Trish groaned in despair.

Oh, God! I wish I didn't love him! I wish I hadn't let
him make love to me...

She tried to cope by forcing herself to picture him at his
wedding, then later with Louise's baby in his arms.

It was then that she realised something awful. They'd
taken no precautions.

She could be pregnant! She gasped, her eyes widening
as she remained rooted to the spot while she considered the
full implications of their carelessness. It was a cruel irony—
a baby, fathered by the man she loved. Wonderful,
but...not like this! She'd imagined marriage, a devoted husband, watching her family grow and...

She let out a wail of anger at herself. God, she was stupid. *Stupid!* Tears ran down her face, mingling with the
warm jets of water, and she shivered from the shock.

'Trish?'

Her hand flew to her mouth at Adam's concerned call,
but she couldn't answer.

'Are you all right?' There was a tap on the shower door.
When she didn't answer immediately, it was yanked open.
Adam took one look at her and caught her wrist, drawing
her out.

'Leave me alone!' she warned shakily.

'Why?'

He sounded very angry. Well, so was she! she thought
as a warm towel was flung over her head and another was
wrapped around her. She stole a resentful glance at him
and saw his hair and his shirt were wet from the shower.
He began to rub her dry and she winced.

'You're hurting!' she complained, her voice muffled
from the concealing folds of the towel.

'You do it, then. But get on with it. You're shivering.
Whatever were you up to?'

'Thinking.' Of a baby, she thought bleakly. Their child.
Her hands began to shake with the awfulness of the
situation.

He made no comment but drew her onto his lap where he patted her dry. Resting her against his chest, he then rough-dried her hair, whereupon she pushed him away, appalled at the strength of her feelings for him.

'I'm going to get dressed,' she muttered, finding it impossible to meet his gaze.

'And explain your reaction,' he said quietly.

Only then did her unnaturally bright eyes flash up to his. '*Explain!* My God, Adam!' she cried. 'Where do I begin? Don't you feel any shame? Regret? Guilt?'

She stalked into her bedroom. He followed. She realised they'd have to talk this over and she steeled herself to face the inevitable embarrassment and his lame excuses. Feeling emotional, she dragged the big bath towel away from her body and flung it into a corner, completely indifferent to the fact that she was naked and his eyes were touring every inch of her. He wouldn't touch her again; she'd see to that. She opened a drawer in the small pine chest and drew out the first items of underclothing she came to.

When she threw him a cold glare, she saw how wet he was, droplets of water dripping from his flattened hair and water puddling around his feet on the cheap carpet.

'You'd better get out of those wet things,' she said curtly. 'And then get your own breakfast and pack.' Her chin jerked up. 'The boat leaves just after ten.'

'You think I should be ashamed,' he said without emotion.

Her eyes widened. 'Only if you have any morals!' she snapped scornfully. 'You've betrayed Louise! How could you forget your fiancée?'

'You know how,' he countered. 'You did. And you forgot yours.'

'But...' That was what came of lying, she thought in exasperation. 'We're not officially engaged. We've known each other for ever. It's taken for granted that we'll marry. It's not the same thing at all.'

'You forgot him, nevertheless.' Taut in every muscle, he

leaned against the dressing table, a foot or so away from her, and folded his arms in a very aggressive way.

Thrown by the truth of that, she struggled into her T-shirt and jeans. 'You—you confused me!' she said feebly.

He snorted. 'And I tied you up too, I suppose? Stopped you from crying out? Be honest with yourself. Admit—'

Trish blanched at his cruelty. 'I'm not used to skilled seducers!' she flung at him defensively, snatching up a hairbrush and tearing it through her tangles.

'So I was good?' he challenged, taunting her.

She licked her lips. Understatement of the year. 'You knew what you were doing. It was wrong,' she said, refusing to answer such a question. 'You've made a proper commitment to Louise and should have kept your hands to yourself.'

'I know that only too well! But you wiped her from my mind!' he said testily. 'What does that tell you?'

'That you're faithless!' she cried. 'How dare you make me take the blame—?'

'I blame you, I blame my reflexes—'

'*Reflexes?*' she yelled, accidentally hitting herself with the hairbrush. She slammed it down, her eyes watering in pain. 'Ye gods! You're blaming your testosterone? Do you do this frequently?'

'No,' he growled. 'Only once before. As you very well know!' Hard-jawed, he reached out, a handkerchief in his hand.

She flinched. 'Don't touch me!' she cried incoherently. 'I suppose it's my fault again! My Spanish blood! What was it you said? Something about the inhabitants of Bryher communing with Nature? This isn't some hippie camp, with free love and nudity, Adam!'

'Well, what do you think it is, what we feel for each other?' he demanded roughly, his gleaming chest rising and falling in fury. 'What shall we call it, Trish?'

'Betrayal!' she cried, her face aflame. 'I have a boyfriend

but I let another man make love to me. You conveniently forgot the woman you're about to marry!'

'I'm not proud of my loss of control.' His gaze swept over her. 'This is terrible,' he said bleakly. 'I should never have gone for second best.'

She felt her body contract with the insult. But he was right. She *was* second best as far as he was concerned.

'You should never have gone for me at all!' she shot at him.

It was her fault as much as his, she thought miserably. Both of them should have controlled their feelings. Adam had disappointed her. He was fickle—an opportunist, taking sex when and where he could find it without thought for the consequences. She felt sick again.

Trish passed a hand over her forehead and stared at her pale, huge-eyed face in the mirror. He'd fallen off the pedestal where she'd placed him. What kind of husband would he make if he could be so easily tempted?

'I didn't set out with that intention,' he said, tight-lipped.

'What did you intend, then?' she demanded.

'You know perfectly well that we've both wanted to kiss and touch one another since we met in London,' he said, his dark eyes accusing her. Trish was stunned into silence. Then her eyes blazed. 'OK,' he said, when it looked as if she might levitate in anger, 'I know what you're saying. That just because you want something it doesn't mean you have to have it. I made a mistake. I didn't know I'd gone too far, before it was too late. For that, I ask your forgiveness—'

'You're not getting it! I don't know how you could treat Louise—and me—like this!' Trish fumed.

'For heaven's sake, Trish!' he said in exasperation. 'Sometimes…sometimes resolutions and promises you make to yourself are impossible to keep.'

'That's a cop-out!' she snapped. 'When you got engaged, you made a choice. Monogamy isn't something you make furniture with, Adam!'

'No—I meant—'

'You have no excuse and you know it!' she raged on. 'Were you after a bit of fun before your wedding? A quick fumble with good old Trish, because you thought she had the hots for you?'

'Trish, don't talk like that!' he cried angrily, catching her roughly by the arms. 'Listen to me,' he ordered. 'You don't understand—'

'I understand only too well!' she stormed, wrenching herself away. 'How can I ever face you again? Or Tim, or Louise? I'm ashamed of myself now. You've ruined everything! I always respected you, Adam! You were always special to me, more caring and less sex-crazy than *younger* men!'

'That's unworthy of you,' he said, white-faced.

But she wanted to plunge the knife in deeper. He'd hurt her. It was his turn to be hurt. 'I don't think so! Now it turns out you're as callous and as casual about relationships as a bunch of young lads out on the pull! You didn't even have the decency to take precautions!'

The blood drained from Adam's face. He looked deeply shocked and Trish realised that he must be worrying about the possible consequences, because he was temporarily speechless. What was he scared of most? she wondered cynically. That she'd claim maintenance and he'd have to tell Louise what he'd done? She could see him shifting on his feet and scornfully supposed that he wanted to get away and put his mistake behind him.

Something sank in her heart and she knew it was the small scrap of hope that she'd nurtured there—a hope that Adam had loved her all this time, and would do the decent thing. Too shaken to stand any longer, she sat on the bed, covered her face with her hands and groaned, loathing her selfishness, sickened by that forlorn hope.

She'd wished misery on another woman. Never in her life had she believed she could consider hurting someone else. Forgive me, Louise, she pleaded with silent vehemence. The woman was blameless and deserved better. Trish slumped in misery, stricken to her stomach with the destructive fall-out from that one misguided surrender to her emotions.

'Trish…' he began, softly, caressingly, as if he meant to get round her.

She stopped him with a glance, unable to bear any silken-tongued excuses. 'You are a rat, Adam Foster!' Her temper suddenly snapped and she picked up the hairbrush and hurled it at him. He ducked. Beside herself with shame and fear for the future, she leapt up and followed it with a hand mirror which smashed against the door behind him. 'Get out!' she screamed, too angry to aim straight. Furious with that failure too, she spat, 'Out!'

Her hand was on her favourite seal ornament. Leaping forward, he snapped his fingers firmly around her wrist and she was saved from hurling it wildly across the bedroom.

'Calm down!' he ordered sharply.

'*Why?*' Her sapphire eyes flashed with anger.

'Because this isn't helping,' he said in exasperation. 'We need to talk—'

'No,' she said firmly. 'I know what you were doing and why. You intended to seduce me. It would have been a brief interlude in your life, nothing more. But for me—'

'Yes?' he asked abruptly.

'Oh, don't flatter yourself!' she scathed. 'I'm talking about the consequences, not the impact of your technique! Don't you see, Adam, how many lives might be damaged—yours, mine, Louise's, Tim's, Gran's…? You've been totally irresponsible—and yes, so have I; I admit my guilt. God knows how terrible I feel!' she cried. 'I wish to God that I'd never met you!'

Slivers of pain flickered across his eyes and she supposed he must be insulted that she was so comprehensively rejecting his lovemaking. There was a long, tense silence. He made no move to comfort her but stood as if paralysed by her remark.

After a while he turned and walked out, with none of his usual vigour, but more like a sick and weary man with no joy left in life.

She listened to every sound he made, picturing him as he stripped off his wet clothes and selected fresh ones, packed, went downstairs and made coffee...and left the house. Her eyes squeezed shut with the pain in her heart. By taking what she'd wanted without stopping to think, she'd given away her own self-respect. It was justice of a sort. She deserved to be hurt. There was no excuse for what they'd done. Never had been, never would be.

And to make sure she remembered her mistake for a long time, the skill of Adam's lovemaking would stay with her always, torturing her unbearably. She bit her lip. She knew that Tim would never caress her like that. Or create such a joyous turmoil in her heart, mind and body that she'd find herself acting instinctively without a thought for the consequences.

Adam belonged to someone else. She would think of him—his smile and his tender, passionate affection—and it would torment her beyond all her worst nightmares. She clenched her teeth together till her jaw hurt, knowing that soon he would be gone. Back to Louise.

Unable to bear the mess she'd made of her life, she consoled herself with the fact that pregnancy after one night was pretty unlikely and she'd only have her guilt to worry about. Burden enough, she thought, gazing sightlessly out to the bay.

It was too early for the boat. Without knowing where he was going, Adam dumped his luggage by the gate and began to walk. Fast and furious. Releasing all the ruthlessly suppressed anger with himself and muddled, conflicting emotions. Past enticing beaches with sand so white it hurt his eyes, along narrow cliff paths above wicked-looking rocks, on and on over the springy turf till the breath began to feel painful in his lungs.

He paused on a dramatic headland overlooking a wide bay, waiting for his heartbeat to subside to its normal rate. Giant rollers roared towards him on the incoming tide, smashing against hidden rocks beneath the water and sending up fountains of white spray.

This must be Hell Bay. Very appropriate, he thought, awed by the elementary forces on display. His fists clenched. He'd blown it. He'd been unbelievably stupid. So much for clearing the field for his relationship with Louise! Arrogantly, he'd imagined his iron control would get him over any little twinges of latent desire. Instead...

He scowled at the turbulent sea which roared and thundered in a spectacular display of raw power. That was it. You didn't fool with natural forces. They had a nasty habit of showing you how puny you were in comparison. Some things, like the tide, you couldn't stop.

As a result, he'd hurt Trish. He thought of her distress—and then, painfully, of her uninhibited responses a few hours earlier. Well, he'd got a result. She clearly despised him and wanted nothing more to do with him. It was the conclusive rejection he'd originally sought. Such was fate. You got what you wanted—when you'd ceased to want it.

His face darkened. If she became pregnant he'd never forgive himself. If only... *No!* Never look back. Never regret. He'd made it a rule not to agonise over the past. Damn Trish and her intense feelings!

Fuming, he continued his walk, unable to remain still. This was where emotions got you. Out on a limb, making mistakes, hurting people.

He could deal with this—and any consequences, should they arise. In the meantime, in all decency he owed it to Louise to discuss their relationship. He'd sort out his life, put it on an even keel again.

The westerly wind blew his hair back and buffeted him hard as if it wanted to throw him off balance. If it did but know, he'd already tumbled headlong. He inhaled deeply. The air smelled sweet and clean and was filled with bird cries. Climbing a small hill, he leant his back against a stone marker. Tresco quay seemed very close. Five minutes by boat. It wouldn't be long before he was there...and then on his way to Louise.

In a habitual gesture, his fingers pressed against his temples. It seemed that his headache had returned.

'Where's that nice man gone?'

Trish switched off the electric cleaner and put on a cheerful face for her grandmother. 'Couldn't stand the frantic pace of life!' she joked brightly. 'Caught the boat this morning.'

'I saw him from Betty's house, up on Watch Hill. He looked grim. Had a row?'

'He's got problems at work,' Trish said shortly, a lump coming into her throat.

'He'll be back.' Unaware of Trish's frown, her grandmother sat herself down, grinning broadly, and turned on the television. 'My favourite chat show! Lovely. A nice cup of tea and a scone would go nicely.'

Trish pulled herself together, kissed the top of her grandmother's head and went to forage in the kitchen.

The next few weeks were busy. And then she had a cancelled booking which meant that both double rooms were empty for a while. Her grandmother suggested she ask Petra to stay, but Trish's two rather plaintive messages on Petra's answering machine were never returned—and suddenly Trish had enough on her plate to cope with.

A female guest had arrived, one who was unusually full of demands. By the time Trish had moved the furniture in accordance with Mrs Varsher's instructions, taken orders for newspapers, magazines and paperbacks, dealt with offending hairs in the basin—extraordinary! Lucy was superfussy!—and returned all the newspapers because, apparently, they were the wrong ones, Trish was in a flat spin.

'Another week before she goes!' she groaned, checking the calendar. And then she froze, seeing the dates and the special marks each month...

She was late. And she was always as regular as clockwork. The figures blurred before her eyes. Feeling faint, she sat down suddenly in a kitchen chair. She was alarmingly overdue. She took a deep breath and told herself that she couldn't be pregnant—not so easily…so soon! Her hand strayed to her flat stomach. She didn't feel any different. Probably nerves, then, or the fact that she kept bursting into tears…

Hell. She'd been snapping at her grandmother, who'd asked her if she was incubating an excess of hormones. Trish grew pale, her eyes huge in her shocked face as the realisation sank in. She *was* carrying Adam's baby, she knew it!

'Feel all right, dear?' enquired her grandmother, pausing by the open garden door. 'You look all peculiar.'

'Bit dizzy—'

'Now, what would have caused that?'

Trish stared guiltily at her grandmother's sweet, concerned face. She couldn't tell her. Quickly she dropped her head so her hair concealed her shame. 'I've been rushing about like a whirlwind after Mrs Varsher,' she said lamely.

She felt her grandmother's comforting hand clasp hers, a soothing stroke on her forehead.

'Don't worry, my duck,' said her grandmother lovingly. 'Stop flapping about. Everything will be all right, you'll see.'

Trish pressed her face against the familiar floral pinny, feeling like a child again, being comforted for the loss of her pet rabbit. Dear Gran. She was always there, always loving.

When she lifted her head, a rueful smile on her lips, she was startled to see that her grandmother's gaze seemed to be fixed on the calendar. Trish tensed up, but apparently the old lady hadn't noticed anything suspicious because she gave Trish a hug and said, 'You young girls! Think you invented trouble! We'll get over this. We always do, always will. How about a nice cup of tea?'

'Lovely,' Trish said, feeling calmer. Of course everything would be all right. Secretively she placed her hand on her stomach, unsure whether she wanted to be pregnant or not. 'No—make that coffee,' she said suddenly, finding she'd gone off the idea of tea.

After a few days, she took a pregnancy test. It confirmed her suspicions. She was carrying Adam's baby. She didn't know what to do—but she had to see Tim, for sure. Edgily she plunged her hands into the sink and began tackling the washing-up.

'Ah. There you are!'

The small, exquisite figure of Mrs Varsher had materialised in the kitchen doorway. Her lovely face was set in discontented lines. Trish wiped her hands and smiled politely, wondering what was wrong now.

'What can I do for you, Mrs Varsher?' she asked, concealing her dread. This woman would find a speck of dirt in the Sahara desert!

'The mattress is stained,' the woman said. 'I want it changed. I'm not happy with your standards of hygiene at all.'

'I don't understand it!' Trish said in bewilderment, following the woman upstairs. 'It's checked after every visitor. There was nothing wrong after the last single occupant—'

'Well, there is now! Look! It's disgusting!'

She was right. An unidentifiable stain had spread across the centre. Trish felt dreadful. 'I'm terribly sorry, Mrs Varsher!' she said unhappily. 'I'll deal with it now.'

It took her a while to heave the mattress out, scrub it and leave it in the sun to dry, then put her own mattress on the guest bed. By the time she'd finished, picked masses of flowers for Mrs Varsher's room by way of an apology and washed up both her own breakfast dishes and her grandmother's, Trish felt she deserved a good walk and a few moments to herself. Feeling frazzled, she left the delighted Lucy in charge of the rest of the cleaning and set off.

Up on Watch Hill, with the stone marker sheltering her from the wind, she idly watched the helicopter heading for the helipad by the Abbey Gardens on Tresco. Then, moodily churning over the revelations she'd soon be making to all and sundry, she walked to the post office to collect Mrs Varsher's papers.

The *Faldore* was already making its way across the channel to Bryher. Remembering with a pang the time it had brought Adam to her, she hurried on to the cliffs above Hangman Island.

Sitting there with the wind ruffling her hair and the sun warm on her face and body, she wondered if he had told Louise about his temporary lapse, or if he'd assuaged his conscience with the aid of champagne, a romantic dinner and a dozen red roses.

Today, without fail, she'd ring Tim. It wasn't fair to keep him in the dark about her feelings, but she wondered how he'd react. He must know what she'd done, yet she shrank from hurting him. Several times she'd picked up the phone and chickened out.

Once she'd seen Tim, she'd need to confirm her pregnancy and tell her grandmother. But not Adam. Poor little baby, she thought sadly. If only things were different—if Adam weren't engaged, if they'd been planning marriage— he'd be overjoyed then, to know she was carrying his child. It would have bonded them together. Instead...

She would bring up her baby alone. Another child without a father. Trish blamed herself, her quick emotions, the ease with which she'd fallen into Adam's arms, like a ripe plum.

With the skirts of her cornflower-blue sundress spread around her, she nestled against her favourite lichen-covered rock and took off her ancient plimsolls so that she could feel the thick tussocks of sea pinks beneath her feet. Wistfully, she stared up at the sky. Here she had everything in the world she could want to possess...other than the man she loved.

Suddenly her beloved Bryher wasn't enough. Her heart had been stolen away and she couldn't feel the same passion for the island any more. London and its gridlocked streets *with* Adam—however flawed he might be—seemed preferable to Bryher without him. It was an extraordinary moment of truth for her.

Everything she had valued so highly was suddenly meaningless. The whole focus of her world had shifted. She would willingly give up her home, her lifestyle and her lifelong friends for Adam's true love.

She frowned, absorbed by the fantasy. Of course she could never leave her grandmother—who was welded to the island by blood and sweat! Then reality surfaced and her mouth grew sullen. Why was she worrying about such things? She'd never be asked to make the choice.

Sad and feeling highly emotional, she struggled to overcome the vacuum which had replaced her heart. It would take time to get over him, she told herself. Early days yet. And she had another person to consider. Her baby. In a gesture which was becoming frequent, she placed her hand where she imagined it must be.

A miracle, she thought sentimentally, smiling for the first time since Adam had left. Perhaps, she mused, ever the optimist, a kind of happiness could come of this. And she began to feel the stirrings of love for the tiny creature growing in her body.

In the meantime, she had to put the washing on, do a batch of baking and mend a fence before lunch!

Trish hurried back over Shipman Head and arrived flushed and panting. A distracted Lucy met her at the back door.

'P-p-p—!'

Calming herself, Trish took the agitated girl's hands. 'Relax,' she said gently. And, remembering Adam, said, 'Try taking a few deep breaths.'

Lucy gestured to the kitchen excitedly, inhaled, and said, 'It's your f-f-f-f—'

Then Trish heard her grandmother's voice, ringing out with its usual blunt clarity.

'...relieved you're here! She's been moping about something awful!'

Trish clutched Lucy in delight. 'Petra? My friend? Oh, Lucy, that's wonderful!'

'I d-d—'

But Trish had hugged the girl and slipped past her, calling happily, 'Petra! I'm here!'

And skidded to a breathless halt.

Not Petra. Adam.

Her bewildered gaze swivelled to her grandmother. Who appeared to be wearing her best hat, the straw one with a huge brim and half of Covent Garden encircling the crown. The one she wore for weddings.

'Why...? What...?' stumbled Trish, going brick-red.

'Lucy came to tell me he'd turned up,' her grandmother said from somewhere beneath the bouncing cherries and blowsy blooms. 'What a surprise!' she said with a suspicious lack of sincerity.

Trish stiffened. Surely her grandmother wouldn't have engineered Adam's return? 'More like a shock,' she said waspishly.

'There I was,' said her grandmother, in tones of amazement, 'in the middle of trying on my—'

'Gran,' she blurted out faintly, before Adam knew the purpose of the hat. She couldn't think what to say. 'I thought it must be Petra,' was all she could come up with.

'Better than that,' said her grandmother. 'I've booked him in for ten days.' She waved a wad of notes at Trish. 'Should be long enough,' she said cryptically.

Trish faced the wary Adam, keeping a rein on her temper for her grandmother's sake—and for that of her own dignity. 'You were taking a chance coming here without checking,' she said coolly. 'I might have been full up— then you'd have been stuck for somewhere to sleep.'

'I don't think so,' he said quietly. 'I'm sure your grandmother would have found me a spare bed.'

Judging by the knowing looks he and her grandmother exchanged, he was right. Trish seethed at his arrogance and knew she couldn't stand living in the same building as him.

He'd have to go. Once she got him on his own, she'd really let rip!

'Time we made ourselves scarce,' said her incorrigible grandmother.

'I'll see you later, Lucy,' Adam murmured, to Trish's astonishment.

Behind her, the girl gasped noisily and said, 'R-r-right!'

Trish turned, amazed. Lucy was beaming at him, her face pink with adoration and pleasure. And Adam... A sharp little knife stabbed in Trish's chest. Only once before had she seen him quite so unguarded, so gentle and vulnerable. They'd been making love at the time.

'Lucy will be making your bed up,' she said tightly, then realised she'd sabotaged her own intentions of turfing Adam out!

'She's done it. Everything's ready for him,' her grandmother said. 'You can't begrudge Lucy this opportunity. Adam's going to teach her how to use a computer! Proper lessons! How about that?'

Trish took a deep breath, cast a quick glance at Lucy's rapt face and knew she couldn't spoil the girl's delight. But when she met Adam's impenetrable gaze she made sure he knew that she was aware of his sly manoeuvring.

'It'll be an excellent skill to have,' she said coolly. 'Excuse me. I have jobs to do.'

'Lucy and I are going to hunt for eggs,' called her grandmother. 'Well, she's hunting, I'm holding the basket. Then, when she's picked strawberries, I'll supervise her making some jam. I'm being discreet. I hope you appreciate that. I know you two will want to be alone—'

'No, we won't!' Trish cried sharply, appalled by the surreptitious glances Adam and her grandmother were sending each other.

There was definitely some collusion going on, she thought grimly. She clenched her fists, cringing at the things her grandmother might have told him. Perhaps he knew she'd cried herself to sleep night after night. That she hadn't been eating. That one day her grandmother had found her curled up in a small, miserable ball in the bed where her baby had been conceived.

She went white with dismay. Adam was the last person on earth she wanted her inner grief exposed to! Why didn't Gran keep out of things she didn't understand?

'We do need to talk,' Adam said, a little tensely. 'You disappear, Mrs Hicks. I'll tell you when you can show your face again.'

Trish's grandmother giggled, not at all offended by his high-handed orders. He's got her wrapped around his little finger! Trish thought hysterically, suddenly horribly nervous now that she and Adam were alone.

She began to fidget. Almost certainly he was aware of her reaction to his departure. That gave him the advantage. Her throat dried as she met his eyes. Disconcerted by their unreadable depths, she let her gaze drop, managing to take in most of him on the way.

This time he was wearing slim-cut jeans and a casual denim shirt with a navy sweater tied carelessly around his shoulders. He looked utterly wonderful.

Unnerved by her covetous thoughts, she took the initiative.

'I'm surprised to see you here.'

'So am I,' he admitted, as if he wasn't too sure he was doing the right thing.

'Why have you come, then?' she asked shakily.

'I have unfinished business.' There was a brief pause. 'You look...well.'

She met his unspoken query with a challenging stare. 'I am.'

He was checking her condition, she thought contemptuously. This was the moment when she should tell him about the baby. But she couldn't. It seemed so bald: *And by the way, I'm pregnant!* She shrank from throwing it casually into the conversation. It was too important to treat lightly, and she needed more time to think out her own feelings before involving Adam—if she ever did. For one thing, it could ruin his relationship with Louise.

She realised that he was speaking to her and she hastily brought her attention back to him.

'...intend to tell you what I've been up to.'

She recoiled, her mouth dropping open in amazement. A blow-by-blow account of his reconciliation with Louise? What did he think she was—a masochist?

'Why should I be interested in your activities?' she asked, quivering with anger and pain. Desperate for something normal to do, she bent down and sorted out the washing.

'You won't know unless you listen,' he told her curtly.

Looking up, she tried to judge his mood. Despite the studied, nonchalant pose he'd adopted, there was something odd about him, as if he faced danger—and was both wary and excited by it. She could feel the vibrations of it now, across the kitchen.

Suddenly a faint smile touched the corners of his mouth and she saw he was eyeing the garment in her hand. Trish glanced down and sighed. Her usual luck was with her. No scarlet panties, lace suspender belt or peek-a-boo bra to make her feel satisfyingly desirable yet annoyingly unattainable oh, no!

'Gran's vest,' she said, daring him to suggest it was more likely hers.

'Warm,' he commented laconically.

'I wouldn't be at all surprised if Captain Oates wore it during his trek to the Pole,' she muttered.

Adam's brief laugh, his beautiful teeth and the warmth in his eyes made her ache with longing. Irritably she grabbed her own small cotton briefs and bras and thrust them into the gaping machine before he saw them too clearly. Her underwear was between her and her body— and no business of anyone else's. She poured in the powder and switched on. Then she washed her hands, turned on the oven and started hauling out of the cupboards everything she needed for baking.

'Couldn't this frantic activity wait?' Adam asked edgily.

'No.' Just as tense herself, she popped an apron over her

head. 'I have a Guest from Hell and I want to make her
something mouth-watering to pacify her—'

'What's hellish about her?' Adam pushed away her fumbling fingers and tied the apron strings in a neat bow.

For a few seconds she was forced to stand still and suffer
the sensation of being charged up by a powerful battery.
Then she was able to put a decent distance between herself
and the battery's source—Adam. Since it was better than
discussing passionate reunions with wronged fiancées, she
told him about Mrs Varsher. He listened and watched while
she agitatedly banged the scone dough about.

'Nothing's right for her,' she finished gloomily. 'I do my
absolute best and she still finds fault. I feel I've failed.'

'She could be doing it deliberately,' he suggested.

Trish's eyes widened. 'No, she wouldn't...' She fell silent. Would she? 'The mattress hadn't been stained the last
time I checked,' she said slowly.

'She could have poured tea over it.'

She nodded—reluctant, though, to believe that someone
would go that far. 'I have to admit that I'm sure I took
down the correct order for the newspapers,' she mused.
'And I can't believe that the basin hadn't been properly
cleaned. Or that Mrs Varsher had asked for coffee after
dinner, not tea. I wrote it down myself...' Her troubled face
lifted to Adam's, her suspicions growing. 'Why would she
behave like this?' she asked, bewildered.

'To get free accommodation,' he said cynically. 'At the
end of her stay she'll list your shortcomings and threaten
to report you to the Tourist Board. You say, "No, no!"
and she suggests she doesn't pay.'

'Oh, hell!'

Trish grimly stamped out the scones and placed them on
a baking tray. It looked as if he might be right! Mulling
this over, she pushed the tray into the oven and began to
collect ingredients for chocolate cake.

'You've got me worried now. If what you say is true,
she could ruin me!' she said anxiously, deftly weighing and
measuring ingredients.

'You've never had anything like this before?'

Beating the eggs and sugar with more than usual energy, she sighed. 'One or two oddballs; nothing I couldn't handle. I usually let Gran loose on the bores and they soon get the message. I've been lectured on Zen Buddhism for three hours, learnt everything there is to know about the under-taking business and bought earplugs for the fellow guests of a couple of honeymooners who spent all day and night in bed. But everyone's always been complimentary.'

Adam rested a comforting hand on her warm, bare arm. She shook it off, aware that they were getting far too friendly again. 'You have nothing to worry about,' he assured her firmly. 'The woman's deliberately creating trouble—'

'But I can't prove it!' she cried in agitation.

'I could help—'

'Leave me to sort this out myself!' she said vehemently. 'You don't have to pretend you care what happens to me. My livelihood doesn't matter to you. You don't give a damn if my guest-house business folds because of adverse reports! But it means a huge chunk of my income vanishing. I can sell eggs and cakes and vegetables, I can cut and tie daffodils in the winter, but we couldn't survive on that. I need this business to keep Gran and me. And...'

He tensed. 'And?' he prompted.

She had been about to say 'And my baby'. Quickly she made a substitution. 'And Lucy.'

Adam gave her a peculiar look. 'Lucy?'

'Yes. There's just her and her brother and he works on the farm next door which is up for sale. He might not have a job this time next year. Lucy will need what she earns from me.' She pushed her hair back anxiously with a floury hand. The future looked tough. 'Adam, I've got enough to worry about without you hanging around. Under the cir-cumstances I'd be grateful if you'd find somewhere else to stay. Give Lucy her lessons, by all means, but have the decency to keep out of my hair. What you do, or have done, is of no interest to me.'

For a moment he watched her adding ingredients, then slamming sponge tins down on the farmhouse table and greasing them as though they were her worst enemies, before filling them with the cake mixture.

'You seem very jumpy,' he said quietly.

He was doing it again. Speaking in that pseudo-special voice. Making her legs turn to mush and forcing her heart to do somersaults. Any minute now and it would be leaping right out of her chest and flinging itself adoringly at his feet. Viciously she snatched up the tins and shoved everything in the oven.

'It's not surprising under the circumstances. I don't know the social etiquette where ex-lovers are concerned! I find this embarrassing in the extreme! It would be easier all round if you pushed off!' she said rudely.

'Not possible. I have unfinished business, remember?'

'Your computer man? I should think he's fed up with hiding behind a sofa in case his millennium bomb goes off!' she muttered.

'You're winding me up!' he drawled.

'No. You're winding *me* up. And I'm about to snap my springs!'

Before he could open his mouth to reply, she was scrabbling in a cupboard for her heavy toolbag, emerging grimly with it and striding across the kitchen in a rattle of saws, chisels and assorted screwdrivers.

'Now what are you doing?' he asked in exasperation.

'I'm either icing a cake or the fence needs mending. You choose,' she threw over her shoulder.

'Leave it for a moment!' he ordered, hot on her heels.

She whirled, confronting him furiously, close to angry tears. 'I will not! You might think it's important to unburden yourself and tell me all about your admission to Louise and the rapturous reunion, but I don't want to know! I've got better things to do. Find a priest if you're that keen to confess your sins.'

Flinging the front door open, she stomped down the garden and dumped her tools by the broken fence.

'Is this vandal damage, the results of your grandmother practising her decapitating-gangsters swing, or mountainous seas?' Adam enquired sarcastically.

Trish scowled. 'Wear and tear. And I'm feeling worn and torn myself, so go away and leave me in peace!'

Feeling horribly bad-tempered, she crouched down, her cornflower-blue skirts settling all around her, and selected a claw-hammer to ease out the wire nails.

To her relief, Adam stopped annoying her with stupid questions and merely irritated her by watching every movement she made, as if he'd never seen anyone mend a fence before.

Oyster-catchers were screaming above Great Porth and she looked across to the nearby beach to see them, registering that they were probably objecting to something which was threatening their nests. Then the danger passed and there was silence. The wind had died down, leaving a blissful peace. Only the sound of the wash of waves on the shore, and terns and redshanks calling to one another, disturbed the serenity.

Adam exhaled with heartfelt pleasure. 'Wonderful to be here again,' he mused to himself, as if the cares of the world were falling from his shoulders. 'Trish, I would prefer to talk to you somewhere private,' he went on decisively, coming to stand close to her. 'But since you insist on fitting me in between your household chores and the DIY, I'll have to make the best of it.'

He appeared to be waiting for a comment from her. She didn't give him one. It annoyed her that he thought she'd be riveted by his actions. Egocentric brute!

Adam inhaled deeply and then exhaled very slowly, speaking on the out breath. 'I've spent a good deal of time with Louise, Trish.'

Not liking the image that conjured up, she kept her gaze fixed rigidly on the paling she was lining up. 'Make yourself useful. Hold the face of the sledgehammer—*there*—like a backstop, so I can bang the nail in. Hold it firmly!'

Placing a nail carefully, Trish gave it a satisfying whack. Then repeated the performance with the second paling.

Adam flung the hammer down grimly. 'That's it. No more avoiding the issue. You'll damn well listen to me!'

'I don't *care* about Louise! If you and she are crawling all over each other, well, that's very jolly. I've got a fence to—'

'The hell with it! A few minutes of your time, that's all I'm asking! It's important to me, Trish. To us!'

'Us? I told you! We don't have any us!' she yelled.

'Why are you shouting?' he asked with enormous interest.

'I'm not shouting!' she snapped, aware how silly that sounded when she felt as if she'd been operating at a volume of a million decibels. She jammed the wire pins between her firmed lips, carpenter-style, to stop herself from saying anything else incriminating.

His eyes glittered and danced. He unpeeled her fingers from the hammer, took the next paling from her hand and then slowly removed each pin. She held her breath. One pin. Two. Three. Four.

His fingers lingered on her lips for several beautiful seconds. And the lowering of his thick lashes and the expression of concentration on his face made her mouth shape itself into an unconsciously sexy pout.

'Do I have your full attention now?' he asked darkly.

She swallowed. 'Yes.' The movement of his hands on her arms was electrifying. Helplessly, Trish looked up. 'Go on.' But to protect herself she added, 'But be quick!'

He gave her a slow smile which brought warmth to his eyes and a tenderness to the lines of his expressive mouth. 'I tried to make a go of it with her,' he said earnestly. 'I thought that was where my duty lay. Almost immediately I realised I was wasting my time. We split up ten days ago. We're not engaged any more.'

Trish's eyes rounded. Her gaze went to his left hand. No ring. A mixture of emotions churned through her. Astonished by his action, she said, 'But surely…if she

loved you she'd forgive you a brief, stupid mistake,
wouldn't she?'

His fingers tightened on her arms. 'Oh, yes,' he agreed.
'I believe she would. But I made it clear it *wasn't* one brief,
stupid mistake.'

'I see!'

Dismay, followed by bitterness, spread across her face.
So he'd behaved like that before, had he? She wasn't the
first! It made sense. He was an out-and-out flirt. If she'd
had any sense she would have realised that. It wasn't likely
that Adam had been tempted only by her! Plenty of other
women would be more beautiful, more seductive and more
riveting companions.

It didn't surprise her that Adam grabbed any woman who
happened to be handy. That was the problem with handsome, madly virile men. They oozed sexuality and needed
constant satisfaction! And weren't risk-takers supposed to
be prone to living dangerously—and born deceivers? She
primmed her mouth in disapproval and returned his intense
gaze with a stony glare.

'You've no morals at all!' she reproved.

'You can't condemn me for facing up to reality,' Adam
said, his expression neutral. 'If I'd really loved her, I
wouldn't look at another woman, let alone be overwhelmed
by the desire to make love to that woman every time I set
eyes on her.'

Trish felt her stomach swoop. His sexual urges had
ruined his future. But then he could hardly expect to have
a lasting relationship and play fast and loose on the side.

'So...it's over?'

'Yes. I don't honestly think it ever got going beyond first
base.'

Why was he telling her this? she wondered. 'Poor
Louise!' she said sympathetically. 'How's she taken it?'

'You sound as if you care,' he said, with some surprise.

'Of course I do!' she said indignantly. 'It's awful to be
rejected.'

His eyes darkened. 'Yes. It is.' He paused as if gathering

his thoughts. 'Louise was very upset. I was surprised,' he admitted, and she was mollified by the concern threading his voice. 'That's why I stayed with her for so long. I didn't think I should go till she'd accepted the situation. She's more vulnerable than you'd think.'

'No,' Trish said quietly. 'You're her vulnerable spot. I saw that the moment I met her.'

'You're perceptive.'

She shrugged. 'The signs were all there.'

Adam frowned. 'She always seemed so cool and composed.'

'We all try to protect our vulnerability, Adam,' she said gently.

He was silent for a moment and seemed to be wrestling with something that troubled him. 'True. It's the only way to survive.'

She realised he'd been thinking aloud and hadn't meant her to hear that. Her pulses quickened. What was it that made him wary of his emotions? The loss of Christine? And now his relationship had foundered. He must be feeling very low.

'I'm sorry it didn't work out,' she said sincerely.

'I wish it had. It all made perfect sense at the time. Now...I know it was a mistake from the beginning.'

'You did the right thing,' she said impulsively. 'You would have made her very unhappy.'

'Knowing that didn't make it any easier to explain,' he said with a frown. 'How do you tell someone you don't love them?'

'The minute you're sure,' she said, feeling guilty about Tim. 'Better that than to keep the other person hoping.'

'I don't think Louise appreciated my frankness,' he said heavily. 'I made it clear that I cared for her, but I felt nothing more than that. She pleaded with me to stay. I spent hours with her, trying to explain that one day she'd meet someone who really adored her and who would walk over hot coals if she asked them to. I did my best to persuade

her she'd be better off without me. It was a long time before
she saw reason—'

'It's the last thing you see when you're mad about someone,' Trish said ruefully.

'God!' he cried with feeling. 'Don't I know that! I've
told myself there are too many differences between us, that
our ages are too far apart, our lives complete opposites, that
I don't want to be overwhelmed by emotional uncertainty...
I'm used to taking risks, but this is ridiculous!' He shook
his head in self-reproach. 'I'm just not listening to sense.
Nothing I tell myself makes any difference. I know I'm
acting illogically but I've no power to stop myself!'

She stiffened. Slowly she turned to stare at him. His hand
caressed her cheek in a gesture both gentle and yet trembling with suppressed passion. It was as if— She jerked
back in alarm, stunned by her whirling, deceiving imagination.

'From...' She hardly dared to ask. But the words spilled
out recklessly, in a husky little voice. 'From what?'

'Wanting you. Being obsessed by you.'

Her hands clasped together convulsively as she searched
his face for confirmation that she'd heard right. Wanting.
Obsession. Her heart thudded rapidly and disappointment
permeated her whole being. It was less than she wanted,
more than she'd expected.

'You can't feel like that about me...' she began weakly.

'I can! God, I can! I've wanted you from that moment
you walked in the door at the age of sixteen, your hair like
black glass, eyes as blue as the sky, a smile on your face
so radiant and joyful that I couldn't breathe for a moment.'

Astonishment softened her mouth as the words tumbled
out in rapid succession. She shook her head in disbelief.
'But...you were so formal and polite—'

'I had to be,' he said, his eyes warm with a heart-
stopping tenderness. 'I felt as if I'd been hit by a train. I
put it down to...well, you can imagine. Lack of sex, emotional hunger, and a need to indulge in a normal relationship... It's none of those—and never was.'

'Christine…' Her throat closed in horror. His wife had been ill and he'd thought only of sex with the nearest available person.

'We never truly loved one another,' he told her in a low voice. 'We had a good marriage based on deep affection. Never passion. I did care for her, Trish. I loathed myself for thinking about you and I denied my feelings for you because of the situation—and because of my regard for Christine.'

'Why did you marry her if you didn't love her?' she demanded, appalled by the terrible lie he'd lived. 'You were only eighteen with the whole of your life ahead of you! It was wrong!'

'Life isn't that simple, Trish! I needed her. Needed someone. She'd been through a messy divorce and had a small child—Petra. We both wanted security, both knew the score. And I was faithful. It was enough till you came along,' he said, jerking out the words in short, sharp bursts of breath. 'I think she knew what I was going through. Several things she said at the time make me almost sure of that—though I refused to talk about you or acknowledge my feelings, even to myself.'

Trish stared at him, stunned. She remembered the conversations with Christine, how the older woman had praised Adam's good qualities, hugged her fondly and said in a joking way—as she'd thought at the time—how Trish and Adam were soul mates.

Then Christine's last words came to her mind. 'Darling, love Trish.' Had that been an attempt to give her blessing to something she'd suspected all along? *Christine knew!* she thought in amazement. Adam's wife had sensed what Trish had felt and was hoping she and Adam would get together in time.

'Christine loved us both,' she began, trying to come to terms with the revelation. 'It was a sentimental hope—'

'It was more than that!' Adam cried roughly. 'She knew us both well. I'd seen her watching us, hoped she hadn't seen the way I was looking at you. But she knew—and she wanted us to feel free to be together. I've only just realised that, Trish. I fought my feelings and tried to forget you. I thought I'd found the ideal wife in Louise because we got on well in the office and shared a common interest in our work... I thought she was all I wanted. I was wrong. Seeing you brought passion back to my life, made me see what I was missing. I want to know everything about you. I am fascinated by all you do. My mind and my body are obsessed with you. No one else and nothing else takes priority. I *told* you, Trish, that I'd made a mistake in going for second best—'

'I—I thought you meant I was second best!' she said in small, strangled tones, staggered—overwhelmed—by his vehemence.

'Not you! Trish—'

He'd slid his hands around to her back. Bewildered, needing space to absorb what he'd said, she ducked away and backed up to the fence.

'What do you want from me?' she wailed, her mind occupied with one thought: that he'd said nothing of love. Incredible though it was, he desired her, she didn't doubt that. That, however, was all he was offering. And she couldn't trust him. There could be no love without trust.

His eyes glittered. 'Everything.'

A moan broke from her lips as an unseen hand seemed to reach in and twist her stomach. It was ironic. This was what she'd longed for. She was on the brink of flinging herself into his arms. It would be so easy to agree. But now she had become more wary. How long would a relationship with him last? He'd soon tire of her. As he'd said, they had little in common. At what stage of her pregnancy—or her child's life—might he take off with someone else who inexplicably obsessed him?

She shivered. The risks were too great. Where once she might have taken the chance, in exchange for precious time with Adam, she had a greater responsibility now. Her baby had made a difference. She must nurture it, protect it and not subject it to a series of failed relationships. She had to be one hundred per cent sure. Nothing less.

'Wanting isn't enough!' she jerked out.

'It is for me,' he said simply, and under his breath added, 'God help me.'

'Lust is no basis for a relationship!' she muttered angrily.

'It's more than that. It always has been. Don't pretend you haven't always wanted me, watched me, come close to me—'

'No!' she whispered, appalled at the terrible accuracy of his accusation.

'I'm the same,' he declared roughly. 'I think of you all the time. Have to touch you, speak to you—'

'But, Adam...I'm all *wrong*—'

'Tell my brain and my body that! I'm in desperate need of an injection of common sense,' he bit out. They stared at one another for a while. Trish's eyes were enormous, her heavy fringe of lashes fluttering in confusion. 'God, you're so...b—' he took a deep breath '—beautiful!' he said, on an outrush of air, as if emotion had robbed him of fluent speech.

She quivered, incredibly weakened by the touching chink in his armour. His eyes bored into hers. He took a step towards her and she found herself unable to move.

'It's madness!' she whispered, wanting it, willing her protest to be overridden. He was free now, she told herself. They might have a chance... Her heart thudded. She, Adam and their baby. All her dreams could come true—if he was genuinely serious. Not otherwise.

'I've had enough of being sensible,' he growled. 'Of wrestling with my conscience and arguing that you should be with younger men—even your boyfriend who doesn't damn well deserve you! I agonise over the fact that you and your perfect, flawless body and enviable youth shouldn't be wasted on a man of my age!' he continued savagely, his entire face suffused with passion. 'I want you, and if all my instincts are right, you want me too.'

'Adam, age doesn't matter to *me* but you surely must want someone sophisticated and—'

'I want you!' he muttered, his unwavering gaze merciless as it pinned her in place. 'I won't listen to anything you say, any objection you put. I don't care what havoc we wreak. I'm beyond all that. If I don't take you in my arms, kiss you, touch you, make love to you, I'll destroy myself with wanting.'

Another step. She felt her legs buckle at his resolve. And then his hands were resting on the fence either side of her body. Trapping her.

'What...are you doing?' she mumbled, breathing only with difficulty.

He studied her for heart-stopping seconds. 'Testing.'

'Testing?' she repeated jerkily.

'The fence.'

Yet, judging from the way he scrutinised her, he was testing something else. Noting the hugeness of her eyes. The trembling of her mouth—and the way it had swollen expectantly. The relaxing of her facial muscles, the tell-tale little catches in her breath, the wild beating of her heart which he surely must hear. She was aware of all those. He must be too.

Now she registered fully the changes in him. This wasn't the Adam she knew. This was someone who'd stripped away all pretence of civilisation, leaving nothing but raw need. An unbending, single-minded Adam, who'd stop at nothing to get what he wanted.

Thrilled and scared, she gazed up at him, transfixed by his resolve. Slowly his lips parted. He remained very still, but energy rippled through him, waiting to be released. Her whole being seemed to be waiting for him to break the intolerable tension between them.

'I want to lay you out on the grass,' he said in a harsh, emotion-charged whisper. 'Feel the softness of your hair between my fingers. Bury my face in that soft skin between your neck and your smooth shoulders and smell your sweetness. Sink my mouth into your breasts and taste each nipple with my tongue. Slide my hands down the curves of your back, mould them around your hips...'

Hoarseness thickened his speech. He paused, swallowing, both of them breathing hard from his words and the intensity of his gaze which had swept over her hair, her throat, shoulders, breasts, taut nipples, waist and hips as he had spoken...

Trish tried to speak. Not a word came from her. Only a small, feral moan sounded in her throat. He wasn't even touching her, she thought, trembling from head to foot in an agony of anticipation. Yet she was aroused in every fibre of her being.

The heat was pouring from her body and it seemed as though she was liquid in each sinew, bone and pore...and deep inside her she could feel the moisture flowing for him, centring her whole concentration on that aching, throbbing core.

An inch or two separated them. It was purely the incredible force field and the extraordinary chemistry between them that kept her his silent and willing prisoner.

'I won't let you reject me again,' Adam said with a soft and ruthless determination. 'I don't care what happens. I can't stay away from you. I think of you all the time.' Suddenly he moved with a swiftness that left her gasping, pulling her masterfully into his arms, locking her to him, his breath warm on her upturned, yearning face as he said raggedly, 'I only want you. To be with you. To laugh and share confidences with you...'

She wilted in his arms, all too easily persuaded, lost to his ardour, wanting all those things he'd spoken of. His hands came up to clasp her head and he bent to kiss her. The sudden hardening of his mouth against hers brought a helplessness so acute that she thought she might faint. And yet...

'No!' she said suddenly, pulling away, her eyes frightened and startled like those of a hunted animal. She was scared of loving him. Loath to be railroaded into surrender and then hurt. 'You can't come back here and pick up where you left off! How do I know your relationship with Louise is over? Maybe you just want someone in your bed while you're over here—'

'Hell, Trish!' he muttered roughly. 'What do I have to do to convince you?'

'I don't know,' she answered with a helpless little movement of her hands. 'I want to believe you...'

She struggled with her conscience. One part of her was urging her to tell him about the baby and secure his commitment. The more sober part was warning her that she could trap them both in a loveless situation which would bring nothing but grief.

She stared at him, trying to weigh him up. He remained stiff and silent, watching her with a wariness that did nothing to ease her suspicions. Was he worried that she'd sussed him out—and that he'd have to find someone else who'd fall for his convincing line of chat?

Look at him, she said to herself. Gorgeous. Rich. Mr International. Get real! Whatever would a man like that want with a woman like you?

His mouth was tightening. It always did that when he didn't get his own way. There was a hardness about his eyes and a quickness in his breathing which surely meant he was annoyed. Well, let him be! she decided.

Knowing she was throwing away a chance in a million, she steadied her own breathing and prepared to tell him she wasn't available for romps in the hay.

He forestalled her, probably reading her body language. 'I'll make you as obsessed with me as I am with you,' he said harshly. 'You will want me. You will need me, I promise you! And now excuse me.' He began to stride away. 'I need to prepare for Lucy,' he called, with a dark, backward glance which chilled her to the bone.

CHAPTER FIVE

As SHE mixed butter cream and spread it on top of the chocolate cake, Trish listened to the sounds from Adam's room: Lucy's squeals of laughter, and his rich voice murmuring so softly that Trish couldn't hear what was being said. Bitterly she realised that he was flirting with Lucy on purpose. He was punishing her. Deliberately, cruelly, exquisitely.

Angrily she cleared up, hating herself for the consuming jealousy that gripped her. At least, she thought miserably, this was proof that she'd made the right decision in turning down Adam's pass. He had no scruples!

She'd have to warn Lucy that he wasn't to be trusted. Adam mustn't repopulate Bryher island all on his own! she thought angrily.

A while later—sixty-nine minutes, she frowned, checking her watch—she heard the phone ring in his room. Apparently it had disturbed them because, shortly after, Adam and Lucy appeared in the kitchen.

Trish took one look at Lucy's brilliant eyes and her flushed, radiant face, and turned away, unable to speak for distress.

'We've made a great start!' declared Adam with satisfaction.

'Hurray,' muttered Trish, shaken by the adoring look which Lucy was beaming towards him.

The girl blushed and shyly left, stuttering her thanks.

'You might have shown some interest!' Adam said testily when she'd gone. 'She's thrilled—'

'So I saw!' Trish snapped, hating herself, hating him.

'Wait a minute!' He whirled her around. 'What's the matter now? What am I supposed to have done?'

'You're fooling around with Lucy!' she hissed. 'Using

110

her! You rat! I could hardly help hearing all that squealing and giggling. Oh, don't pretend!' she fumed, when he stared at her in astonishment. 'You were trying to make me jealous, to—'

Adam froze. He caught Trish's arms and turned her to face him. 'I wouldn't be that spiteful!' he said angrily. 'Do you really think I'm like that? You know that Lucy is terminally shy! How am I to teach her anything if she doesn't relax? I typed a few jokes on the computer. Got her to communicate with me on screen. She was ecstatic, Trish! For the first time in her life she was able to have a normal conversation!'

'You…you were laughing…' she said uncertainly, startled that he was so genuinely shocked by her accusation. Was she wrong? He seemed so offended…

'Yes, we laughed. She's damn funny! And she went away on wings! You saw her. I *know* how she felt! Don't you realise what it meant to her, to feel like a normal human being for once?'

Trish swallowed, upset that her paranoia over Adam had made her jump to the wrong conclusion. 'I'm terribly sorry,' she said humbly. 'You stormed off, saying you'd make me want you… I thought—'

'There are plenty of ways I can prove that I'm serious about you without involving Lucy,' he said quietly.

She hung her head. 'Please, please forgive me! I believed all kinds of dreadful things about you. I've been very stupid.' She lifted her face, tears of distress in her eyes. 'Thank you for helping Lucy.' Her voice wavered. 'You've done more for her in a short time than I have in months. You're very kind and thoughtful and I'm terribly grateful to you for going to all this trouble. I care about Lucy. I wish I could take back everything I said, all the things I thought!' she mumbled, close to tears.

He sighed. 'I wish you'd trust me, Trish. I'm doing my best to show you how committed I am. Hey! Don't cry!' he crooned, when she began to sniff. He took her in his arms and laid her head against his chest, stroking her hair.

After a few moments, when she sounded calmer, he gently kissed the top of her head. 'I hate to see you cry,' he said huskily.

She looked up and he kissed her salty mouth with great tenderness. She'd been a fool. He did care. 'Oh, Adam!' she breathed, lifting her arms and kissing him hard.

Briefly he responded, then pushed her away with an expression of regret. 'I shouldn't be here,' he said ruefully. 'I've just had a call saying that some parcels are waiting for me at the quay—and they'll need picking up immediately. Wait there,' he said, kissing the tip of her upturned nose. 'Wait there, my darling, and I'll be back before you know it.'

She smiled, watching him hurry away. He'd called her his darling. Gleefully she hugged herself, and skipped around the kitchen. Darling. Perhaps... She paused. Adam found it hard to acknowledge his emotions. He'd just made a huge step in calling her that. Maybe he couldn't say the 'L' word—yet. But it might only be a matter of time.

Then she'd tell him about their baby. He'd be stunned at first, then his face would break into a grin of pride and he'd hold her tightly—no, carefully—and—

Her fantasies were interrupted by a weird noise coming from upstairs—one of his machines. Hurrying up, still dreamily thinking of the wonderful moment when Adam would know he was going to be a father, she pushed open his bedroom door. Nothing was wrong at all. A fax message was chattering its way out of his portable computer.

She was about to leave when her eye was caught by a picture of wedding bells on the scrolling paper. Something made her stop and retrace her steps. Curious, she bent to read the message... She froze in horror.

It was from Louise. She was asking Adam to vet the cover of the Order of Service—for their wedding.

The phone rang loudly, startling Trish so much that she jumped. Trembling, she picked it up. 'Yes?' she said in a tight little voice.

'This is Louise. I'm checking that Adam's got my fax—

oh, and that he's picking up the wedding invitations and
colour charts and fabrics for our new house.'

Trish sat down heavily on his bed, all the air expelled
from her lungs. She licked her dry lips and tried to control
her voice but it came out croakily, nevertheless. 'You—you
and Adam are...getting married?' she jerked out.

'Well, you knew that! You came to our engagement
party!' declared Louise.

'I thought you'd split up!' Trish gasped.

'I don't know what you're talking about,' Louise said
coldly. 'Adam and I have just spent some wonderful weeks
together!'

Struck dumb by that, Trish dropped the phone back on
the cradle, staring at it sightlessly. Several minutes went by
until she felt able to move. With limbs as heavy as lead,
she got up and tore off the fax, reading it again, her trembling lips moving silently as she prayed for a miracle, for
the words to be transformed into something different.

Darling, what do you think of this? Wedding bells!
Divine, aren't they? Give me the OK and I'll go ahead.
Adored Paris—you rascal! Can't wait till you come back.
Thanks for the roses. Thirty! Deliciously extravagant!
Adore you... Louise. XXX.

Her eyes closed in pain. He had deceived her. Oh, she
couldn't bear it, this joy and sorrow, soaring to the heights
of happiness and the depths of despair! Better to know
nothing but ordinary, plodding things than to experience
such agonising see-saw emotions!

She sat there trembling, steeling her heart to him, peeling
away the layers of love and affection he'd so unjustifiably
earned. Maybe he *had* been fooling around with Lucy! she
thought. She wouldn't put it past him now!

As for telling him her news... No! Not *ever*! she vowed;
he didn't deserve to know. She didn't want a man like him
having anything to do with her baby! She became all
choked up, mourning the man she'd thought he was, feeling

only contempt for the shallow, pleasure-seeking person he'd hidden from her all this time.

Carefully, she folded the fax and slipped it into her jeans pocket. At some stage she would confront him with it. Perhaps even lead him up the garden path for a while, then, when he was in the middle of some out-and-out lie, she could calmly produce the fax and ask him very sweetly to give her the address of the house he and Louise were doing up, so that she could send a house-warming card.

When he returned, she was unnaturally calm and looked up from polishing the sitting-room bookcase with a smile of enquiry on her face.

'Nothing there,' he said with a puzzled frown. 'No parcels, nothing.'

'How odd,' she marvelled caustically, thanking fate for the mix-up. If he hadn't been called away she might never have known he was still engaged!

'Annoying to have been interrupted,' he murmured, heading for her.

Then she heard something that alerted all her senses, a sound which she'd been unconsciously listening out for. And it stopped her dead in her tracks.

'Adam!' she breathed, forgetting everything in her panic. 'I think Gran's fallen!'

Without waiting to see if he followed, she sped towards her grandmother's cottage, hearing Adam close behind her. They both exchanged startled glances when a terrible, guttural cry rang out.

'What's that?' he cried in horror.

'Lucy! Trying to call for help. Something's badly wrong!' she wailed.

He accelerated, Lucy's desperate gargle becoming more frantic. In a moment he had overtaken Trish, his long, loping strides quickly covering the distance to the open doorway.

When she arrived a moment later, wide-eyed and breathless, it was to see Adam crouching by her grandmother, who was lying awkwardly on the slate floor of the kitchen.

Lucy was cradling the old woman's head in her lap and he seemed to be gently but urgently persuading her grandmother to cautiously test out the movement in her limbs.

'Oh, Gran—Gran, darling!' cried Trish, sinking to the ground and taking one swollen-knuckled hand in hers, everything forgotten but her concern.

'I'm all right. Stop fussing, you lot!' grumbled her grandmother. 'Ouch! That's my arm you're making free with, young man! Go and play with one of your own!'

But, although her words were jaunty, the shake in her voice and the whiteness of her face told another story. Trish leapt up and grabbed the shock remedies from her first-aid box.

'Open,' she ordered, hiding her own distress and releasing a couple of drops onto her grandmother's tongue.

'I think there's probably a break in that arm,' Adam said quietly. 'She ought to be checked over—'

'They don't do anything for fractures nowadays,' muttered the old woman. 'We might as well rely on the good old-fashioned methods.'

'That'll be Symphytum. Knitbone,' explained Trish, seeing Adam's frown.

His brows drew harder together as if he disapproved. She remembered Stephen's scorn when she'd dosed herself with the age-old Ignatia remedy for grief, just before Christine's funeral. Now Adam was proudly supporting his son's career in conventional medicine. He'd probably think she was weird too. It was another example of the gulf that existed between her way of life and Adam's. They were a lifestyle apart.

'Just get me to a chair,' said her grandmother. 'It's my own fault. I was wearing my hat and I didn't see that I'd dropped some strawberries on the floor. I slipped.' Her eyelids drooped.

'Don't go to sleep!' said Adam sharply, his hand quickly feeling through the white curls. He exchanged glances with Trish and mouthed, 'Bruise.'

Trish kissed her grandmother's wrinkled cheek. 'Hospital

for you, like it or not,' she said perkily. 'Handsome doctors
with cold hands, attentive nurses with enemas—you'll love
it, you know you will!' She saw the glimmer of a smile on
the worryingly pale mouth, administered the shock remedies again and then checked her watch, uttering a groan
of dismay. 'No boat!'

Adam's mouth thinned in suppressed exasperation. 'Now
what do we do?' he asked, scowling at her.

'I'll have to ring Joe Slater. He's the neighbouring
farmer,' she explained as she rose and started dialling.
'He's got a small launch in Stinking Porth, the next bay.
He'll take us to St Mary's.'

'Right. Lucy,' Adam said urgently, taking control again,
'find some blankets for Mrs Hicks. Then go next door and
get my thick jacket from my room, and something for Trish
to wear. It'll be cold on the water when we come back.
We'll both go to the hospital. Can you manage dinner for
Mrs Varsher tonight on your own?'

Lucy nodded and Adam eased the old woman's head into
the solid warmth of his chest. Trish finished explaining the
situation to Joe and knelt beside her grandmother again,
alert for any hint of concussion.

'He'll prepare the boat immediately,' she said shakily.
Her eyes took in Adam's white face. The hospital, she
thought at once. It must be bringing back memories of the
hospice. Despite her anger with him, sympathy flooded her
heart. 'Look…you don't have to come, Adam—'

'I do.' Their eyes met over her grandmother's head. He
managed a crooked smile. 'Someone has to carry your
grandmother to the boat—and from it, if need be. And it
could be late before you return. I might be needed on the
return journey.' He touched her hand, caught it in his and
gave it a reassuring squeeze. Her eyes were dark and pained
as she drew her hand away. He seemed so tender! she
thought miserably. 'She'll be all right. Don't worry,' he
said consolingly.

'Don't mind me!' muttered Trish's grandmother. 'Do
your courting over my head while I try to die quietly and

not bother you!' But she was smiling, Trish could see, even through her own tear-filled eyes.

'Die quietly? Huh! We should be so lucky!' Adam drawled, with a teasing grin.

'Rascal!' muttered the old woman, giving him an approving pat.

Adam knew that, since he was a stranger to the dangerous waters around the Scillies, he couldn't pilot the launch himself despite his skill at handling boats. Instead, he made it his job to cradle the uncomplaining Mrs Hicks securely against his body for the long journey to St Mary's. Somehow both he and Trish managed to keep her conscious with a teasing repartee that had even the reserved Joe smiling.

The tide was low and Joe pronounced Tresco Flats virtually impassable, so they went the long way, around Samson island. Adam vowed to buy a nautical chart and learn the waters. He didn't intend to stay an ignorant city man for long. It wasn't in his nature to feel as helpless in an emergency as he had with this one.

Throughout the journey he noticed a cold rigidity about Trish, and a heartbreaking tremble of her lower lip. She tried to control it for her grandmother's sake, making little jokes about doctors and nurses till he yearned to gather her up and hold her tightly in his arms.

Why? he raged silently. Why even consider involving himself with someone who was so deeply passionate, so open and defenceless that she could get hurt? And thus hurt him, remind him of the agonies he'd gone through...

'Adam.'

He focused on her. She seemed to be a blur. He couldn't speak. So he lifted an eyebrow enquiringly.

'Do you have your mobile phone with you?' she asked anxiously. 'We could ring ahead. I know the number.'

Curtly, he nodded and handed it to her. He knew he was afraid of her concern, her unbounded ability to love, feel compassion, pain. Perhaps she was the one with the greatest courage.

His pulses quickened as they came closer to the hospital. If he'd had any choice he would have excused himself and waited in the boat. But he was needed. A hospital car met them on the quay. Flashbacks kept springing into his head. Sam. Moaning. His own voice yelling. Sam's face. God! Sam's face...

'Are you all right?' came Trish's soft, low voice.

A dumb nod with a grimace. Then a swallow to clear his throat of the choking ball that blocked it. 'Headache,' he lied hoarsely.

After a moment's hesitation, she stroked his forehead, massaging his temples with her cool, gentle fingers. Then she pressed her thumbs hard beneath the bones at the base of his skull. He concentrated his mind on what she was doing and the images faded.

It was getting worse. Trish was opening him up to things best left forgotten. He couldn't live without her...yet he feared to live with her. Her lack of faith in him had been unexpected—it was as if she knew that he wasn't being entirely honest with her about Lucy.

Perhaps her grandmother was wrong about Trish's feelings. He wanted Trish so much that he might be into wish-fulfilment here and that was blinding him to the truth.

He went pale, thinking how appalled he'd been at Mrs Hicks's heavy hint on the phone that Trish might be pregnant. At least that seemed unlikely. If she was wrong about that, she could be wrong about everything.

He ought to walk away. Leave his emotions intact. The uncertainty, this to-ing and fro-ing of uninhibited abandon and total rejection, was wrecking his smooth, ordered life. He tipped his head back, closing his eyes, knowing he craved her like an addict. He must convince her that he cared because he couldn't go on like this much longer, desperately finding ways to subdue his hunger for her.

'We're here.'

Touched by Trish's croaky little voice, he squeezed her

hand. 'Everything will be OK now,' he said, wishing she weren't drawing away from him as if he'd burned her with a branding iron.

Being worried about Trish took his mind off being in a hospital again. Her grandmother was taken immediately for X-rays and they were left to cool their heels in the hospital corridor, clutching paper cups of a liquid which claimed to be tea.

'Think I'll go and see my mate Bill,' Joe muttered, evidently ill at ease in his surroundings. 'Give him a jerk up. Farm lease is for sale,' he added, seeing Adam's puzzled expression.

'Yes. Trish mentioned it,' he said politely. 'I gather it belongs to the Duchy of Cornwall.'

'Whole of Scilly is Duchy land. Belonged to all the heirs to the throne since the first Prince of Wales, Duke of Cornwall, in 1337,' Joe said proudly. 'Bill's supposed to have two people interested. Give us a call when you're ready to go back. It's only across the beach.' Joe recited the number and Adam wrote it on a card in his wallet.

Waiting dispiritedly on the chair he'd found for her, Trish looked exhausted, her mouth drooping with distress. His heart lurched with affection and he sat next to her, his arm coming comfortingly around her shoulders.

'Don't,' she muttered, shrugging it away. 'I can't cope with that.'

'I want to look after you,' he said gently. 'At this precise moment, I want to wrap you up in cotton wool—to protect you from any harm, anything sad or bad or mad!'

She turned, her beautiful eyes soft with worry. Seeing she would be too weary to resist, he kissed her cheek, marvelling at its texture, aching to hold her very, very tightly and build a wall around her so she would never know what it was to be hurt.

'It would be difficult to get my storm coat on,' she observed, her voice still quite shaky. He sat close to her and could feel the trembling throughout her body. 'And having a shower would be a n-nightm-m...'

Tears were coursing down her face. Pain seared through his heart. His brother had cried like this. Adam let the pain roll through him. He'd been helpless then as well. Emotion prevented him from speaking. He just reached out and held her, stroking her hair in silent agony, grateful that she let him.

He was beginning to care too deeply. It was unbearable seeing Trish so unhappy. 'Don't cry,' he muttered hoarsely, only just stopping himself from stuttering. Cursing himself, he got a grip and blanked out that night he'd held Sam like this, while the tears had coursed down his own face and mingled with his brother's. 'Don't worry,' he soothed in Trish's small ear. 'It'll be all right.'

'I love her so much!' she sobbed into his shoulder, her muffled voice wrenching at his heart. 'She's been wonderful to me! You see why I worry about her—she will dance about in those sloppy slippers of hers and forget she's none too safe on her pins. And she *would* wear that hat!' she wailed, as if that were her fault. 'Gran's all I've got—'

'No,' he said gently. 'You have me too. You will have me for as long as you want me.'

Trish raised a tear-stained face. He smiled at her and wiped the damp streaks with his handkerchief. From the way she was looking at him—puzzled, confused, stunned and disbelieving—it seemed that she hadn't taken on board what he'd been trying to tell her.

'No. You don't! You—'

'Leave it for now,' he advised, easing her back into his arms and drawing her resisting head to his shoulder, persisting till she gave in and slumped heavily against him. He wanted to win her over but knew that wouldn't happen overnight.

'It took me six years to work it out,' he went on. 'I don't expect you to start coping with the potential problems of our relationship right at this moment. I know you feel passionately about me. That's a start. It's enough for the time being.'

Absently, he kissed her warm scalp. She smelt of a

herb…rosemary. He wondered if she used it to shampoo
her hair. There was so much he wanted to know. A lifetime
of knowing.

'Gran depends on me,' she mumbled wearily against his
throat, her words sending shivers over his skin. 'I can't ever
leave her.'

Tipping up her chin, he looked her solemnly in the eyes
and said, 'I'm not sure I could, either! I'm only interested
in you because she's part of the package too.'

Trish didn't laugh, as he'd hoped she might. 'You've
been very kind to her,' she said, with a heartrending shake
of her voice. 'I…' She seemed to be struggling with con-
tradictory emotions. 'I'm glad you came, Adam!' she said,
albeit a little stiffly.

He held that simple, wonderful phrase to him, throughout
the waiting, Trish's emotional reunion with her grandmother, and the journey back late that evening, during
which he quietly assured Trish that her grandmother would
be fine, the doctor had said so, and they were only keeping
her in overnight as a precautionary measure.

Eventually Trish's lashes fluttered down to rest thickly
on her cheeks and he left her wedged in the small cabin to
sleep. He and Joe had things to discuss.

Trish reluctantly emerged from a wonderful dream. She and
Adam and her grandmother were seeing two children off
to school on the Tresco boat. Her children. Adam's. They
waved merrily to the blue-clad figures and trudged back up
the hill to…

That was when she woke. Her mouth pinched in as reality hammered itself into her thick skull. In a few years'
time he'd be waving merrily to his neatly uniformed children as they alighted from his Bentley and walked sedately
into their prep school. Then he'd go off to his hermetically
sealed office, hurl faxes and gigabytes in all directions and
return to the perfectly preserved Louise for cocktails and a
trendy dinner for twenty intimate friends.

Six o'clock. She scrambled out of bed and went to the

bathroom. Then the events of the day before came rushing back. Gran! How was she? Was it too early to ring?

And… Her hand went to her mouth. Who had put her into her pyjamas? The last thing she'd known was falling asleep…on the boat! Cautiously her hand went downwards to check. No knickers!

A flame of red swept over her face and she whirled around. There they were, neatly placed on the chair beside the bed. With her bra. The sundress had been thoughtfully hung on one of the padded satin hangers she'd made.

Trish dressed herself, fed the chickens and laid the tables for breakfast. All the time she did so, she was trying to ignore the trickles of excitement which had invaded her bloodstream. He had touched her body. Looked at it. Maybe allowed his hands to linger…

She gulped, disturbed and dismayed by her wicked delight. And rang the hospital.

'She's fine,' the staff nurse said cheerfully. 'Sitting up and demanding a doctor with cold hands and her enema.'

Trish giggled with relief. 'My fault! I threatened her with that to make her laugh. When can we collect her?'

'I think she should stay for a day or two. Her blood pressure's sky-high and, cold hands and enemas apart, she seems confused. Keeps talking about strawberry jam and wedding hats.'

'It makes sense to me,' Trish said hurriedly, looking up as Adam wandered in. She frowned, surprised by the sinister-looking clothes he was wearing and the extraordinary hairstyle he'd adopted. Then she gave her attention to the nurse again. 'Well, if you're sure she's enjoying herself… Yes, she's in love with all the doctors on *ER*,' she said wryly. 'Warn the hospital staff, or one of them'll find himself on honeymoon with her before he knows what's hit him…Yes,' she said, her voice softening. 'Tell her we'll come this afternoon. Thanks. Give her our love. Bye.'

'Thank you for including me.'

Trish blinked. It had been automatic. Suddenly she felt awkward. 'Gran's fine,' she said noncommittally.

'I'm very glad,' he said, giving her a very intent and puzzled look. She put the table between them. 'Last night,' she ventured nervously. 'Did you...undress me?'

Adam smiled slowly as if remembering something warm and delightful. 'I carried you to your bedroom. Placed you on the bed...'

Her eyes glued to his, Trish gulped and said breathlessly, 'Yes?'

'Lucy did the rest. She was waiting for us to return.'

'Oh.' Relief ran through her in ripples. 'That was kind of her.'

'She's a jewel,' he agreed. 'Such a lovely girl.'

Trish nodded. 'Beautiful. With a lovely nature, too.'

'Great legs.'

'Oh, fantastic,' she said, with lessening enthusiasm for this conversation. Her suspicions were growing.

'Fabulous blonde hair—'

'Yes!' she snapped.

Adam's grin told her that he'd teased her deliberately. He seemed very pleased with her reaction and she flushed, annoyed that she'd risen to his bait.

'I gather from the expression on Lucy's face when I enquired,' he remarked idly, 'that Mrs Varsher was vile to her.'

Instantly worried, Trish bit her lip. 'I've got to do something about that,' she said anxiously.

'It's already in hand,' he said, waiting till she'd run a puzzled glance over his black shirt and jeans, and the jacket slung Italian-style around his shoulders. To say nothing of the black curls cascading onto his forehead. At least he'd stopped short of a gold medallion, she thought, suddenly doubting his dress sense.

'What are you up to?' she asked, not sure that she liked him muscling in on her problems.

'Tell me this, first. Is Mrs Varsher a TV engineer in her spare time?'

'Don't be silly! Of course not!'

'Then why,' Adam murmured, 'do you think she was fiddling with the back of the TV set in her bedroom?'

'I've no idea!' Almost immediately, one struck her. 'You don't think—'

'No. I don't *think*. I know.' He took a pen from the dresser and scribbled something on a piece of paper, then tucked it in a cereal packet. 'Play along with me,' he said, a glittering light of battle in his eyes. 'We'll get rid of the woman without any trouble. Any chance of breakfast? I'm starving.'

He'd finished his eggs and bacon and was well into his second round of toast when Mrs Varsher came down the stairs and stalked into the small conservatory.

'Buon giorno!' Adam called smoothly, with a highly continental wave of his hand.

Trish came to a dead halt in the doorway, her own greeting dying on her lips as she watched Mrs Varsher deal with the lowering, narrow-eyed assessment coming from the rather menacing 'Italian'. Then, as the woman muttered a wary 'Morning!', Trish twigged. Adam meant to be intimidating. Hastily, she closed her opened mouth, unpopped her eyes and assumed an air of normality.

'Good morning, Mrs Varsher!' she trilled merrily.

'It's not!' the woman snapped.

'Momento, cara.' In a sinuous, snake-hipped movement which had both women goggling, Adam slid from his seat and came to Trish's side. 'My woman,' he said, in a breath-taking knee-trembler accent, 'she say…you not happy—'

'I certainly am not!' cried Mrs Varsher heatedly. 'This morning—'

'Ah! More things is wrong?' Adam asked with silken menace, puffing out his chest.

'Yes. They is. Are!' The woman dragged her gaze from Adam and addressed Trish directly. 'My television's packed up. Nothing in this place works! It's a disgrace! I don't expect to pay for such bad service and appalling accommodation and hygiene—'

'Signora,' purred Adam in satin tones, 'please to look in

the box and to read to me what is in there.' He pointed to the cereal packet.

Irritably, the woman opened the top and drew out a piece of paper. '"The *Signora*..."' She paused and shot a quick, mystified glance at Adam.

'*Continuez.*'

Trish jammed her lips together hard, hoping the woman would be so dazed by Adam's scary scowl that she wouldn't notice he'd wandered into the French language by mistake.

Apparently she didn't, because she turned back to the note and did as instructed. '"...will pretend that the television in her bedroom..."' Scarlet-faced, she read on silently, apparently too shocked to wonder why Adam could write, but not speak, perfect English. The note fluttered to the table. Her eyes swivelled to Adam's.

By this time he had left Trish's side, his hands were on the table and he was bending forward, clearly simmering with righteous indignation.

'I see you. I see what you do to the TV. My woman, she not happy. I not happy. Is bad,' he snarled with a terrifyingly sinister hiss through his clenched teeth. He brought his face to within a few inches of Mrs Varsher's. 'You tell the lies. I do not like this. In my country, peoples like you have bad accidents. You unnerstand?'

The woman nodded dumbly. She understood. Trish held her breath, thinking drily that people in his country had bad accents, too!

'So,' murmured Adam. 'You go now. Huh? You pay what you owe and we say goodbye.'

'I can't! I—my cheque-book's in my beauty box and...and the combination lock is jammed!' stuttered Mrs Varsher.

'Show me! I, Valentino Capelli, will rip it open with my bare hands!' Adam declared dramatically, all macho biceps and flashing teeth.

Trish ran into the kitchen before she exposed their fraud by collapsing on the floor in peals of laughter. She choked her way into a towel, hearing Adam's menacingly murmuring voice and Mrs Varsher's increasingly high-pitched squeals. What *was* he doing—other than overacting?

A while later, she heard them at the front door and peeped into the hallway. Adam's dark, threatening bulk filled the opening. She crept up behind him and saw Mrs Varsher on the track to the quay, dragging along her heavy case, a dress bag, her vanity box and several carrier bags. It would be a long and tiring haul—but Trish didn't care!

Adam's hand came up. Between his finger and thumb was a cheque.

'Is good, no?' he murmured.

Despite herself, Trish began to laugh and so did he.

'Peoples have bad accidents! Oh, Valentino Capelli!'

'Eh, my woman, she happy?' he said, in a terrible imitation of someone who'd been rightly rejected for a part in *The Godfather*.

Trish just laughed till the tears rolled down her face. 'You were hysterical! You ham! I wanted to burst out laughing! How did you stay so serious?'

'Because it was serious, sweetheart,' he said, his grin fading a little. 'She was causing you grief. No one does that...*and lives*!' he cried, reverting to his role for a ridiculously flamboyant moment.

He's so convincing, she thought with sudden bitterness. Charming, funny, utterly plausible. 'Thanks,' she said grudgingly. And added with cynical truth, 'You were brilliant.'

'Now,' he said, catching her waist with both hands, 'we're alone. No more guests, Trish. You and me—'

'It won't stay like that for long!' she said quickly, moving away. 'I have guests coming in soon. I need to earn a living.'

'But, for now, we can be alone and see where our relationship takes us,' he said persuasively. His voice lowered to a throaty caress. 'So, *cara*! Where were we? Somewhere interesting, I'm sure—'

'No, Adam!' But he was kissing her, stroking her lips

with his tongue, and she felt the heat swirl and begin to overtake her again. Was sex all he wanted? she asked herself distractedly as her mouth devoured his frantically. *Whatever was she doing?* Aghast, she pushed hard against his chest. 'No! I can't. I must see Tim!'

His eyes narrowed. 'What for?'

'To talk to him. About our relationship.'

She was unnerved by the intensity of his expression. It was the tough-guy clothes, she told herself.

Adam's eyes glittered in his dark face. 'You don't love him!' he declared.

Jealousy, she thought. He wants to possess me utterly. It made her feel frightened. He would like to dominate her, rule her every movement, and destroy her independence. Love seemed so wonderful in films. The truth was that it made you feel as if you were balancing on the brink of a precipice with uncertainties nibbling away at the edge.

'It's taking you a long time to agree!' he muttered. 'Let me remind you of something...'

His mouth was everywhere: her lips, face, throat, shoulders... Fierce and sweet, generating a terrible physical longing, it instantly brought the response he'd wanted. Her anguished groan. Her struggle against the acceptance of his hands, easing down her zip. Her treacherous desire to strain for a greater closeness.

She lifted lids heavy with languor. His eyes were brilliant with a savage need, darker than she'd ever seen them. She felt her breasts being caressed and lifted, the stroke of his fingers across the agonisingly hard peaks.

'Say you don't love him!' he whispered with a biting insistence.

'I don't!' she gasped. 'Please, Adam! Don't... This isn't fair!'

'You want rules?' he growled, bending his head and brushing her breasts with his mouth. 'There aren't any!'

She shook with wanting. He shot her a look of such hunger that she felt as if her bones had melted. Then he was tugging at her nipple with his teeth, filling her with rocketing spasms which increased in urgency as he nursed at her breast with ecstasy in every line of his face.

He couldn't stop himself. Knew this wasn't what he'd planned—that he'd meant to court her, make her fall for him, show her that his feelings involved more than sex, and thus remain in control. But again and again he had only to touch, kiss, *think* of making love to her, and his desire was unstoppable.

It was hot. Too hot for clothes. He was kissing her, caressing her, shedding his shirt, drawing her dress from her incredible body. And then there she was: in just a pair of briefs, huge-eyed, scared but aroused and making every inch of his body feel alive.

She was so lovely. Her skin glowed. Her hands were clutching at his hair, sweeping around the curve of his head. And now she was making urgent little cries which almost made him totally lose his head and take her there and then.

Somehow, God knew how, he stood there, skin to her skin, marvelling at the crashing of his heart and the helter-skelter pounding of hers. Her mouth was doing wonderful things to his collar bone. Nibbling. Sucking. The sensuality of her body was driving him wild, inviting his hands to stroke and knead and torment in their turn.

He knew that, until they had made love again, neither of them would be satisfied. There would be no sanity, no means of knowing if this was just lust or a deeper emotion. Yet he sensed that it would be more than a physical act, that he'd be pulled more securely into her web. And so he ought to be walking away for his own good.

He groaned, catching at her, making her move against him as his mouth claimed hers. This headlong desire, this craving for her, to touch and taste and smell the warm scents of her body—these were alarming signs of his dependency on her. He'd always been in control of his life. Trish threatened to make him weak, to tug at his heartstrings.

No! he thought, racked with pain. He couldn't let that happen.

'But...Adam,' she moaned miserably. 'We can't.'

He lifted his head. His senses reeled from the softness of her skin, the elusive perfume of her hair. But. Yes, there were a thousand 'buts'. Before he lost all reason again, he took advantage of her doubts and thrust her back blindly.

Breathing hard, he slowly began to focus his gaze. There was an angry darkness in her face, a rigidity about her slender, voluptuous body. Damp black curls clung to her forehead and he ruthlessly suppressed the urge to kiss each one.

'But.'

It seemed that she couldn't get her breath and that it had caught in her throat. Several times she swallowed, and each time he wanted to take her in his arms and love her with all the passion in his imprisoned heart.

'I—must—see Tim!' Her liquefied blue eyes pleaded with his.

'I agree. I suggest now would be a good time!' he said curtly, bending, fumbling, and handing her the discarded dress with an accusing stare.

Awkwardly she struggled into it. He didn't help her, but bit his lip at the ache which came when her body was clothed again. Deprivation made his eyes glitter with hard lights.

'Now isn't possible. You can't do what you want when you want, here!' she said jerkily. 'I have to clear up. Breakfast things—'

'The world won't come to an end if you leave them!' he said, hating himself for his savagery, knowing its source. Desire and fear. He was shaking. This was more than physical need or romantic love. It could be destructive, ripping apart his carefully constructed life—and he didn't know how the hell to deal with the two opposing needs: the satisfaction of his senses versus survival.

'I might as well,' she said shortly, staring at a point

somewhere over his bare shoulder. 'There isn't a boat till lunchtime.'

'Damn this place!' He could hear himself and couldn't stop. The frustration was too much. 'You'd think that living on an island would be total freedom. It's not! It's like being in a prison!'

Trish flinched, the shudder rippling throughout her body. Cold as ice, she moved to pass him. And he let her. He had to examine his feelings. Cool down. Work out what the hell was happening to him. When he'd flown back after hearing how distressed she'd been without him, he'd been crazy with joy.

He'd never imagined that he'd feel so threatened by the intensity of his emotions. Never in his whole life did he want to feel vulnerable again. And with Trish he was in danger of being just that.

The sound of Trish stacking crockery came to his ears. He opened the front door and walked out into the sunshine.

CHAPTER SIX

THE dishes received a ferocious scrubbing. It was that or weep and Trish wasn't the sort to buckle under.

Damn him! she cursed. Angrily she scoured a spatula. He'd been furious when she'd stopped him making love to her. He'd neither cared for nor considered Louise and, because of his sublime indifference to his commitment, Trish had almost been swept along by his passion again.

A small tear welled up at the corner of her eye and she brushed it away impatiently. It was an obsession of Adam's, this determination to seduce her. He was a dangerous philanderer with the morals of an alley cat.

And he hated Bryher. Loathed its restrictions. He must go back to where he belonged.

But all the while she cleaned and tidied, her body's needs mocked her. She kept pausing, her eyes drowsy with memory: the sensation of his lips closing around her swollen nipples, the warm smell of his hair and the hardness of his aroused body...

She was standing transfixed, her eyes dilated with sexual images, when he walked in. Her breathing quickened. They looked at one another, helpless and fevered in an instant. Matches to a flame.

Sun gleamed on his head, giving it a sheen of polished ebony. She saw his brittle mouth, the tenseness of his jaw and clenched hands, and loathed herself because all she wanted to do was run to him and kiss his muscles into pliancy.

Instead she meticulously arranged the tablecloth in her hand on the kitchen table and smoothed out non-existent wrinkles.

'The boat'll be at the Bar in half an hour,' she said stiltedly.

'The Bar?' His brows met. 'At the hotel?'

'No.'

Trish looked around the immaculate kitchen for something to do. There seemed to be nothing left to tidy, so she watered the geraniums on the window sill. Again. The excess water ran out of the saucer and overflowed onto the sill. She mopped it up irritably and saw he was waiting for a clarification of her remark.

'When the tide's low,' she said in stilted tones, 'the quay can't be used. We use the long jetty—Anneka's Quay—at the Bar.'

'Trish,' he said quietly, 'I'd like to come. Not to see Tim, of course,' he added quickly, seeing the protest forming on her lips. 'To have a look round St Mary's. Say hello to your grandmother.'

'I can't stop you from catching the boat and going wherever you like. I'm going to freshen up. I'll show you where to go,' she said stiffly, and fled.

He sat alone in the prow of the *Faldore* staring sightlessly out to sea. Disturbed by his remote silence, she went into the pilot's cabin and chatted with Ken, carefully fielding questions about the tall, dark and brooding stranger who'd accompanied her.

They clambered up the steps to the quay on St Mary's and walked without speaking towards the small town.

'The tourist office is up there,' she said, as if to a stranger. 'They'll explain where the hospital is. We'll meet there.' Awkwardly she added, 'Gran will be pleased to see you.' He nodded curtly and she gabbled on nervously. 'Tim works in the Jumping Jack Gift Shop. I suggest you don't go in there.'

'I won't. Not my scene.' He hesitated. 'I know this won't be easy for you, Trish—'

'It has to be done. I don't love him. He needs to know so he can get on with his life.'

'I know that. Don't be upset.'

He touched her arm briefly and then strode away. She

watched his vigorous body, the hint of tension in the way
he carried himself. With a sigh, she set off up towards the
small town. As she approached the gift shop, her pulse
began to race. But the shop was empty. After two sharp
thumps on the counter bell, Tim emerged from the back,
his hair dishevelled, a handkerchief rubbing at his mouth.

Just as Trish was about to greet him, his assistant followed. She was from the mainland and had arrived for the
summer season. Apparently for some fun. Her lipstick was
smeared and her brief top sat slightly askew. Trish stared
in amazement.

'Hi!' said Tim, flushing to the roots of his ash-blond hair.

Trish was struck dumb by his infidelity. Then she remembered that she too had been unfaithful. Under the assistant's hostile gaze, Trish walked forward and took Tim's
hands in hers.

'It's OK,' she said, feeling suddenly free. 'I don't mind.
We drifted into our relationship, didn't we? Have fun—'

'No!' he protested. 'Don't be like that!'

'We were never great lovers,' she said fondly. 'We've
always been able to live without each other, haven't we?
That's not love.'

'Maybe not,' he conceded. 'No. It's not.' He smiled at
her. Then his eyes narrowed in concern. 'Is there someone
else?'

She hesitated. It would be easier if she said there was.
'Someone who claims he's crazy about me...' she began
wryly.

'All men are liars, darling,' drawled the assistant with a
cynical sneer. 'They think about sex every ten seconds. Put
a willing bird in front of a guy and we know what'll happen.'

Trish's clear eyes met the young woman's. A chill settled
around her heart.

'Don't get hurt, Trish,' Tim said quietly, virtually echoing Adam's words.

She smiled. 'I'll try not to,' she promised, with a light-
ness she didn't feel.

Adam had the power to break her heart. To hurt her, physically, mentally, emotionally. She knew what miseries her mother had been through because of her father's lack of fidelity. Adam was bad news and she must get him to pack his bags as soon as possible.

She saw Tim and the woman waiting patiently for her to go. 'Keep in touch,' she said affectionately.

'Will do. Take care,' Tim said, with a friendly smile. His assistant placed her arm around his waist. He grinned at Trish and she saw him imperceptibly shift his hip against the woman's.

Trish walked out. The confrontation had been easier than she'd expected. But Tim's behaviour had shaken her. He hadn't seemed the type. Solid, unimaginative, reliable...

Perhaps, she thought with a sigh, he'd thought the same of her. Who could be trusted where sex was concerned? Not even her, with her high standards of morality. Certainly not Tim or Adam.

As she walked through Hugh Town, greeting old friends and exchanging pleasantries, she thought how much her life had changed. She wasn't the same person. Adam had turned her whole world upside down, teaching her things about herself she never knew existed.

She craved sex. Wanted only to be near Adam, to see him, hear his voice. Her face darkened. It wasn't a feeling she liked and she had to do something to cure herself.

When they returned from the hospital, she handed him Louise's fax. He read it with an expression of growing astonishment.

'She's lying!' he said hoarsely. 'Trish, you don't believe this?'

'It seems rather an elaborate hoax for anyone to make,' she said, her face set like stone.

His eyes closed in pain. 'I'll kill her!' he muttered. Then he strode towards Trish and gave her a little shake. 'When did you see this?'

'You'd gone off to the quay to pick something up,' she said sullenly.

'Something that wasn't there,' he growled. 'She set this up! Rang me, put on a false voice and sent me off on a wild-goose chase, hoping you'd be around to hear the fax—'

'She rang—'

'I bet she did! How else could she make doubly sure you heard her lies?' he said, fixing her with his penetrating gaze. 'I told her what I felt for you. She's being spiteful. I swear to you I'm telling you the truth! I'm not engaged to Louise. I want to be with you. Dammit, Trish, can't you see that, in everything I do? The way I look at you, take care of you...'

He stopped, his voice shaking uncontrollably. And she wavered too, seeing how close he was to desperation. He picked up the phone and dialled. 'Louise,' he said curtly, his eyes black with anger. 'Get off my back! Nothing will tear me away from Trish, do you hear? And either you speak to her now and tell her the truth about our engagement, or I'll sue you for slander and for grossly mismanaging my business, and you'll not only be broke but you'll never work in the City again!' There was a pause while he listened tensely, and then he handed the receiver to Trish.

Louise was crying. 'Please, don't be upset,' Trish said unhappily.

'Upset? You little cow! You took him away! He was mine, mine, do you hear?' Louise screamed.

Then Trish knew that the relationship was over, that it had been over for a while. For a moment she let Louise rant on, and when she'd admitted that they were no longer engaged Trish put the phone down.

Adam gave a huge intake of breath. 'I think we should talk. Over dinner. I'll book it. Excuse me. I've got to sort my head out,' he said huskily, and walked up to his room.

Trish sat down and began to think in earnest. So he was free. They could be together. She tried to visualise that and failed. For all his declarations, Adam was totally unsuited

for life on Bryher. What would he do? Feed the chickens
and help her to bake cookies? He'd die of boredom. They'd
be at each other's throats in two months. Then he'd leave,
like her father—who'd been even less of a city man than
Adam.

And her heart would break.

But she wanted him. Her hunger was getting in the way
of rational thought, undermining every sensible decision
she made. He had only to look at her with those sexy eyes
and he could do what he liked with her.

Unless... She stopped. Dug her teeth into her lower lip
hard. No. She couldn't. The thought clamoured persistently
in her head. Let his desire burn itself out. Seduce him, it
whispered enticingly. If that's all he wants, he'll go. And
you'll be well shot of him...and with a fabulous week or
two to remember.

She was wearing a low-necked white cotton dress with a
full skirt and an eye-catching bodice which pushed up her
breasts provocatively. He did his best to keep his gaze on
his plate of curried prawns and occasionally the view from
the hotel dining room across the beach, but it wasn't easy.

'You're very quiet,' she said, her eyes unnaturally bright.

He gave a perfunctory smile, snapped off a piece of
spiced garlic popadam and took a great interest in the bird
life. 'Thinking about work,' he lied, deciding that a few
hours battling with a new program he'd been creating might
keep his mind off Trish's glorious body.

She leaned forward. He could smell the delicate fragrance drifting from between her breasts, tantalising his
nostrils. 'Is there really a guy on Bryher, waiting for you
to defuse his time bomb?' she asked earnestly.

'No. But I didn't lie,' he said, before she could accuse
him of doing so. 'I only said there could be someone like
that here.'

'So...there's no reason to keep you here.'

'Only you. You were my unfinished business.'

'You could leave tomorrow, then.'

'When I have what I came for.'

She seemed satisfied with his response.

He met her warm blue eyes and felt himself drowning. There was something different about her this evening. A special radiance. And... Her mouth curled into a teasing little smile. Adam tensed. That had been pure, sexual promise.

What did it matter? a little voice said inside him. Taking her to bed again might solve all your problems. Then came a more reasoned argument, one he'd decided on a while ago. That he'd only remain untouched if he continually ensured his head ruled his heart and body and he kept her at arm's length till she trusted him and he could trust her. It was like a battle. Mind over matter. Lose command, and go under.

'If...' Her fingers toyed with the stem of the wineglass, mesmerising him. Muscles tightened throughout the whole of his body as his wayward mind threw up images of her long, artistic fingers stroking him. 'If you're not doing anything in the morning,' she said softly, 'you won't mind if I have a lie-in?'

Driven crazy by the rise and fall of her breasts, he shrugged, gave what he hoped was an easy smile, and fixed his gaze on the boats outside which had been pulled up on the springy turf.

All through the meal, she seemed dreamy and slow, her voice ravishingly husky. He hardly knew what he'd eaten, though he was sure the pheasant had been excellent. It appalled him that the only thing he wanted to do was to get her back to the cottage and into bed.

'You're scowling,' she said, touching his hand lightly. 'I see you're not interested in your pudding. Shall we go to the lounge for coffee?'

Without waiting for his agreement, she wiped her beautiful mouth with her napkin and made to rise. The habit of a lifetime had him pulling out her chair before he'd reflected on the wisdom of being so near to her.

Alarmingly, she turned, a pulsating inch or so away.

'Lovely meal, Adam. Thank you for suggesting it. I do appreciate someone else's cooking.'

'My pleasure,' he murmured, wondering wildly what the diners would think if he caught hold of her curving waist and kissed that succulent pink mouth.

Before he could risk finding out, she turned and swayed through the dining room. Everyone's eyes were on her and he felt absurdly proud. For a moment, she paused to chat with one of the waitresses she knew and, after she'd introduced him to the witty, amusing Karen, he watched her laughing and joking, her eyes dancing with fun. The whole of Trish's seductive body was relaxed from the wine and her gestures were fluid and graceful. He couldn't keep his eyes off her.

He'd got it bad. But he'd be a fool to make love to her without some kind of commitment on her part. She hadn't said she loved him. Her doubts were plain to see. No sex till then. Oh, hell!

They helped themselves to coffee and little pastries and sat in blue tartan chairs by small-paned windows, overlooking the lake. Behind it, the sea idled in the evening light, the skyline a hard navy blue.

'We'll see the sunset from here,' Trish murmured, crossing her legs with a heart-stopping exposure of silken thigh.

It occurred to him that the sunset might be a cliché, but at least it meant he didn't have to stare at her inviting legs. The sunset would be a convenient device to keep his pulses under control.

'Terrific,' he said, with a shade too much enthusiasm. Swallows were swooping over the lake, dipping occasionally to the smooth surface. He tried to look as if the scene had captured his attention completely. 'What's that bird?'

'Water rail!' she cried excitedly. 'Clever you! Wait…' Leaning forward, she picked up a pair of binoculars, which had been left by a guest or thoughtful management, and put them to her eyes.

Unobserved, he was able to study her for several seconds. The curl of her dark hair around her tiny ears. The sweet line of her throat. The swell of her honey-coloured, flawless breasts. He could look at her for the rest of his life and not grow tired. For ever and always he'd find delight in that gentle smile, the eager way she sat, like a child awaiting a treat—when all she was seeing was some vaguely rare bird...

'Adam? Adam!' She laughed when he started, and came over to him, sitting on the edge of the easy chair. 'I said, Did you want to look?' To his concern, she retained the binoculars around her neck and bent close, intimately so. As he reached up to take them, she murmured, 'It's kind of nocturnal. Can you see it?'

He muttered something, conscious only of her body against his. After a brief moment of pretending to look at the wretched bird, he passed the binoculars back.

'You...you weren't really interested, were you?' she said in disappointment, going back to her seat.

He felt a heel. She cared that he should find bird-watching as fascinating as she did. Maybe he would, but not with the kind of competition it was getting tonight!

'Sorry. My thoughts were elsewhere.' He gave her an apologetic smile and she seemed content.

That was what he liked about her. She didn't nag or whine or sulk. In fact she... Desperately, he fought with his emotions. Afraid of being split in two by his feelings, ripped apart by them—

'What's the matter, Adam?'

He looked at her lovely face, the anxious deep blue eyes beneath dusky lashes. 'Nothing.'

'You had such an odd expression,' she said quietly. 'What were you thinking?'

'That you're the most beautiful—' His eyes flickered. He hadn't meant to say that, but it had come from somewhere in his subconscious. So instead of adding 'woman in the world', like some adoring newly-wed, he made the statement sound less important. And finished with, 'Woman in the room.'

She looked at him gravely, then cast a quick glance around the room. 'Thanks.'

Seeing that—other than two elderly ladies in the corner—she was the *only* woman in the room, that wasn't very flattering. He grinned and she smiled back, not at all annoyed. He could have hugged her for that.

'Shall we go back before I think of any more clumsy compliments?' he suggested, making light of his gaffe. 'Or would you like some more?'

'You can flatter me outrageously the whole of the way home as a penance,' she told him with a laugh.

Once outside, she shivered in the cool air and rubbed her bare arms. 'Haven't you brought anything to keep you warm?' he asked in surprise.

Her dark eyes slanted to his, feral, panther-like. 'There's you.'

Tightness gripped his throat. 'Sure.' He began to shrug off his jacket but she stopped him and drew his arm around her.

'Hold me.'

How could he resist that soft plea? They stood hip to hip on Gweal Hill, watching the sun sink in the west. With the gentle wash of the waves on the rocks below, champagne air in his lungs and the warmth of the woman he loved by his side, he thought he'd never been so happy.

It was natural that they should turn and kiss when the last vibrant glow of the balled sun disappeared into the blood-red sea. Natural that it should be gentle and sweet and utterly loving. He wanted to stand there for ever, tasting her satin lips and the faint fragrance of almond from the little petits fours they'd eaten.

He didn't hurry. They had all the time in the world. He kissed her cheeks, her closed eyes, suppressed a shudder at the rapture of her expression and came back to her mouth because its sensuality was driving him mad, had fascinated and absorbed him from the first time he'd seen her.

This time he'd stay cool. OK, he was already aroused. But he had an iron will. And he needed it if he was to win her trust and love without fear of finding himself her prisoner.

'Time we went back, I think,' he said, when she began to return his kisses too passionately.

'Yes,' she breathed, her eyes sparkling like diamonds.

Adam tensed. She was expecting him to take her to bed. Wanted him to. Protecting himself, he made conversation as they walked with arms around one another towards the cottage.

'I thought I'd go to the mainland tomorrow. Bit of business,' he said, preoccupied with the luminosity of her face.

'You can't,' she replied, her slender frame inexplicably rigid from head to toe. 'It's Sunday. There's no transport on a Sunday.'

'None?' he cried in amazement.

'No. And if you're expecting Sunday papers you'll be disappointed. They come on Monday. And if the weather's too bad for the helicopter they don't arrive till the *Scillonian* docks at lunchtime. Is that a problem?'

'I can go on Monday,' he said, puzzled by her sudden sharpness. 'And I think I'll live without the Sunday papers.'

Trish pulled away, visibly upset now. 'You need the bustle and excitement of city life, don't you? Even Truro was too small a city for your tastes. You had to move to London—'

'I moved, sweetheart, because I wanted to get away from the memories in my house.' He stopped her, gently turned her to him. 'Memories of you, Trish. That's why I relocated. I don't know what it's like to live somewhere like this. But I want to try. You may think I'm rushing off eagerly to inhale a lungful of polluted air and taste the delights of traffic jams again, but I have to sort out with Louise how we slice up the business—however angry I might be with her. There are practicalities to consider. She is my partner, remember.'

'Oh. I thought... Me. You left because of *me*?' She lifted a bewildered face, which he cradled lovingly in his hands.

'Listen, Trish. We'll have a trade. I tell you something

about myself and you tell me why you looked like you were sucking a lemon when I said I wanted to leave the island.'

She giggled. 'Deal.'

He kissed her small, perfect nose, pleased they were making progress. 'When you left that time four years ago, I felt devastated. I don't know what I'd been expecting or planning, but my subconscious must have believed you'd be there for ever. And suddenly, because I'd behaved like a kid grabbing sweets, you'd gone.'

He paused, his mind filled with other memories, another loneliness. But he'd been younger then, and his heart had been unprotected. Gritting his teeth, he closed the door on his teenage grief.

'I thought you'd kissed me because you'd needed someone to hold,' she said quietly. 'I left because I was ashamed of encouraging you at such a time.'

'I kissed you because I'd wanted to for some time and because I didn't have my usual grip on my emotions,' he corrected her. 'My only regret is that I didn't tell you how I felt at the time. I missed you more than I could have imagined. The house was empty without you. I spent long, endless days and nights working. Neglecting Stephen. Pushing Petra away. It was her idea that I should move to London. And soon I was so busy that you faded into the background and I was caught up in the excitement of making my software business one of the best in the country. Work is a good substitute for a relationship, Trish. I lived for my work and didn't even notice that I felt stressed out. I prefer it here. I promise you.'

She turned her face to kiss his cradling hands, then snuggled into his chest, her head tucked beneath his chin. Suddenly she gave him an involuntary hug.

'I'm glad you appreciate Bryher,' she said huskily. 'I had you down as a striped shirt and pinstripe type, stuck on the M25 with a mobile phone grafted onto one ear.'

Laughing at the painfully accurate image she'd painted, he stroked her hair absently, staring out into the thick velvet darkness, the stars intensely bright in the black sky.

Listening to the silence. Inhaling nothing but pure air. There was nothing between them and America except a few wave-battered rocks, and that gave him a sense of awe.

'I'm not looking forward to leaving Bryher even for a day or so,' he admitted. 'I'll be relieved to return.'

To his surprise, she swivelled around and put her arms around his neck, her eyes alight with joy. 'You couldn't have said anything to please me more,' she whispered, drawing his mouth down to hers.

'I'm sure I could think of one or two things,' he said drily, gently pushing her back. 'Now you tell me why you tighten up when I make plans to visit the mainland. It's more than a horror of missing my ugly face, isn't it?'

'Much more,' she agreed soberly. 'It's the curse of Scillonians. They meet a mainlander and he or she thinks island life is no different from what they've been used to— but with more water. That's not true. There's more to it than that and we're wary of people who claim to have fallen in love with our way of life.'

'I'm interested in you. Where you live is irrelevant,' he was careful to point out.

'It's not. I'd almost rather you'd discovered a passion for Bryher first,' she said with a sigh. 'Take my father, for instance. He came from the mainland, Adam. He was always slipping off, seeing old friends. He felt trapped here. Then one day he phoned to say that he'd found someone else in Plymouth and he wanted a divorce. Mum was devastated.'

He stroked her cheek with the side of his finger, his heart going out to her. 'And you think that any guy from the mainland is likely to do the same.'

'I'm realistic,' she replied. 'I don't expect anything of you. It's a very different way of life and hard to adjust to.'

'I'll give it a try.' He kissed her unhappy mouth and somehow restrained himself from promising more. 'I know you'd never leave Bryher. So I'm intending to see what it's like being an islander. I want to prove that I can stay the course.'

She sighed, her eyes closing in bliss. So he kissed them. Smiling, she said ruefully, 'How can anyone ever be sure they can trust someone?'

'By their behaviour over a period of time,' he replied. God, he was stern with himself! He'd wanted to say, In bed and by flinging aside all defences. But he wasn't that stupid. So he fabricated a yawn. 'I'm tired! All this sea air. I have some work to do on my computer in my room and then I'll have an early night, I think. Hope I don't disturb you, tapping away.'

Trish wondered why her attempted vamping had failed. After some promising signs early in the evening, he'd gone off the boil. The first thing he'd done when they'd walked into her cottage was to heave a sigh of relief and ask if he could make some cocoa.

Cocoa! She'd stood in the kitchen, all tricked out in her sexiest little number, oozing bosom and legs, and he'd pottered around chirping on about bracing walks and learning the difference between whelks and limpets!

Flinging off her Mata Hari outfit, which included her prettiest pair of briefs, she grumpily flopped down on her bed. They'd made some progress, she conceded. He'd claimed that he had every intention of staying. But could she believe him?

Hot and restless, she turned and thumped the pillow for the twentieth time. It was no good. She'd never sleep. Cocoa called.

By the light of the moon, casting its silvery light through the open window, she slipped across the room. Her naked body was reflected in the mirror, shocking her with its unfamiliar voluptuousness. Before she knew what she was doing, her hands were smoothing the incurvation of her waist and shaping the swell of her hips.

Her lips had parted, her breasts were already springing into urgent life and she wanted Adam to enjoy her; she could see that in every fluid line and the brilliant sheen in her eyes.

Angry with herself, she dragged her threadbare old robe around her and tiptoed down the stairs. Suddenly cocoa didn't appeal. Her body needed to do something violently physical to erase the terrible longing.

She flung the front door open. Cool air whispered over her body. Without stopping to put on shoes, she ran out to the beach. There, in the heavy silence, she shed her robe and took a deep breath before running headlong into the sea.

It hit her nakedness like a wall of ice. Undaunted, she gasped, tensed and struck out, revelling in the feel of the silky black water on her skin. Laughing, exhilarated, she rolled onto her back and floated, marvelling at the great black canvas above and the stars, winking at her wickedness.

Something nearby caught her eye. She came upright and doggy-paddled, but it had disappeared. *A seal!* she thought in delight, giggling at the story it would have to tell when it returned to its chums!

'God, Trish! Why—?'

Trish whirled around in a flurry of foam. 'Adam!' she squeaked, her mouth drying in an instant at the thought of being so dangerously near him and so totally nude. Not a seal, but Adam, water streaming from his bare shoulders, his skin gleaming in the moonlight! She ducked down till waves lapped her chin. How much had he seen?

He began again. 'Why did you have to do this?' he asked raggedly.

'I…wanted a swim!' she replied, bewildered by the question.

'Why?'

Her eyes flashed. 'Isn't that perfectly obvious?' she flung recklessly. 'I'm tired of pussy-footing about! I did my best to lure you into my bed and you turned me down! Now I'm cooling off. OK?'

Adam licked his lips involuntarily. 'You…' He steadied his breathing with an effort. 'This is going to sound like a silly question, but…why would you want to lure me into your bed? You're not the sort for a casual affair…'

'I thought it would test my theory.'

'Ah. You have a theory.'

'Yes,' she said, pushing back her wet hair defiantly. 'I thought that if you only needed sex from me, then… then…'

'Then we'd sleep together, I'd realise it wasn't a real obsession at all but only unfulfilled lust, and I'd go home on the next boat, perfectly satisfied.'

She nodded. It sounded stupid. 'Something like that.'

'What if,' he murmured, his eyes as dark as the sea, 'the sex continued to be so good that I wanted more? Would it bother you if it turned out to be pure lust?' he asked quietly.

Her mouth twisted with pain and she didn't hide it. He had to know how she felt. 'Are you that blind, Adam?' she whispered.

There was a hushed silence between them. She felt the love pouring from her in an unstoppable flow. And his face became drowsy with sensuality.

'We took a risk once before,' he said with difficulty. 'We can't be that irresponsible again—'

'It's all right,' she said softly, smiling, thinking of the moment when she would tell him her news. Her heart lifted in anticipation. 'You needn't worry.'

He let out a huge breath. 'Then come here, mermaid,' he said thickly.

She couldn't move at all. She watched him coming towards her and she lifted her head proudly, then she stood up, exposing her naked breasts. Adam drew in a strangled breath and devoured her with his eyes.

'Some men search for sensual experiences,' he said softly, droplets of water clinging to his dark lashes. 'Some have them thrust upon them.'

With his glittering gaze fixed on hers, he moved towards her, and she to him. The sea lifted her to him, offering her. Without a thought for the consequences, she raised her arms to his neck and caressed each tiny divided slick of hair at his nape. Water acted like an oil, lubricating the slip of his hands over her back and buttocks. She closed her eyes, gasping as he cupped each round cheek and brought her hard against his pelvis.

Tenderly, she cupped his face, kissed his salty mouth, and licked it hungrily. Their tongues locked, tangled, tasted, mimicking the act of love with a sweet intensity that made her totally forget everything but her need for Adam.

She slid against him, lithe and sensual, her eyes never leaving his. And then he was twisting her around, pulling her into him so that her back lay against his torso. His legs kicked strongly and they were floating, she on top of him, moaning from the erotic brush of his fingers across her breasts.

She dared not move. Didn't want to. The sensation of weightlessness, and the fact of being adrift in the naked night with him, added to her arousal. Where the sea had seemed cold, it now cradled them in gentle warmth. A far greater heat had taken over her body...and his.

Beneath her buttocks, a ridge of heat throbbed its demands. Inside her was a molten core, getting hotter and hotter with every delicate, minute squeeze of her nipples between his finger and thumb.

'Adam, Adam!' she breathed in desperation.

'What is it, my darling?' he whispered hotly in her ear.

'I can't stand it any more!'

'Sweetheart!' he muttered.

He gently eased her down till she felt the sand beneath her feet. But only for a moment. His hands caught her in their strong grasp and she was being lifted, carried aloft as he strode out of the sea and across the beach. He kept kissing her, his beautiful head dipping to her mouth, her throat, her breasts...till she felt she might die of longing.

She felt herself being lowered and there was the smell of camomile being crushed by her body, the evocative fragrance wafting all around her. Adam's body covered hers. She surrendered herself to his mouth, crying aloud with the desperation of her wanting.

Soft, savage little sounds came from his throat as he suckled her lower lip. Trish fought him, her body incapable of waiting.

'Adam!' It was a trembling, agonised moan of complaint, which he stifled with his mouth as they rolled onto their sides. And she fought him again. 'Touch me!' she ordered furiously, her eyes blazing into his. 'Touch me, Adam! Now!'

For a moment she thought he would thrust her away. His eyes were so dilated they were almost all black and there was a twist of pain to his mouth. Her hands slid between their bodies, down, down to the small triangle of paler skin. Daringly, she caressed him there. And she felt a wonderful triumph when his eyes closed and his lips parted in a groan of sheer delight.

He was beautiful. Hot satin. Frighteningly powerful. Not caring what she did, she slid languidly down his body, letting her hair brush the tip of him. To and fro, to and fro. She knew from the tension in him and the pounding of his hand on the ground that this was an unbearable sweetness. So she did it again, overjoyed that she was pleasing him.

But he hauled her up. 'Enough!' he said thickly. 'Stop! I'm only mortal, for God's sake, Trish!'

Her eyes silvered in the moonlight and she looked at him from under her lashes. 'I love you. Love me,' she whispered into his mouth. 'Love me...'

He groaned. The sound came from deep inside him and with it came the total surrender of his body to hers.

The touch of his fingers shocked her with its gentleness. And she was astounded by the havoc it could wreak in her body. So delicate a movement, she thought hazily, and yet it brought such indescribable pleasure! She gave herself up to it, writhed and luxuriated in the wonderful sensations chasing through every part of her, her hands reaching out to clench handfuls of the camomile turf as Adam wrought his magic.

Their skin was almost dry now in the warm night. Only the slickness of her desire remained. Feeling beautiful and loved, Trish raised her arms over her head and arched her body, every movement and the expression in her drugged eyes saying...*now*.

The moment he entered her, gentle but insistent, she shuddered and clutched him speechlessly. She loved him. Adored him. Worshipped him. With her mind and body and soul. Flames began to lick through her, muzziness obliterated her thoughts and then there was nothing but Adam's body filling hers, claiming her for his own and driving her closer and closer to the edge of rapture.

Over and over again waves of sensation crashed through her, and she let herself drown under their onslaught as they raised her body up to a crest and then sank her down to a fathomless blackness, darker, more enveloping than the deepest sea.

And then she became sleepily aware that her body was no longer being tossed about by a storm, but was floating beneath Adam's again.

'Sweetheart,' he murmured. Shifting his weight, he laid his head on the turf beside her.

She smiled, too shattered to speak, too overwhelmed by the exquisite feelings in her body. And far too shaken to put her incredible happiness into words.

'I think we should go to bed,' he said, some time later, waking her from a deep sleep.

'Mmm.'

It was wonderful to be lifted, carried and placed gently on Adam's bed. Indescribable to feel the warmth of him against her back and the soft whisper of the sheet as he pulled it over them both. She felt cherished.

'Sleep well,' he whispered, kissing her cheek.

She smiled again in deep contentment. 'Mmm!'

Adam laughed fondly and cuddled up to her, his whole body relaxing as if it contained no bones at all. And soon he slept while she remained awake for a short time, revelling in the feel of him, the fact that he was there. And that they had made spectacular, unforgettable love.

CHAPTER SEVEN

AT DAWN Trish woke, enjoying the deep satisfaction which filled her whole body. Her hand reached out…and encountered an empty space.

She looked about her cautiously. A chill ran through her. Adam was sitting in the window and something about the quality of his stillness made her heart pound with alarm. Explanations for his tension raced through her head.

He was having regrets. He'd discovered that he didn't want her any more. She went white. It had been her fault. She'd wanted to know, one way or the other. And now she did. Because men who used women for sex were notoriously quick to distance themselves afterwards. Wham, bam, thank you, ma'am, she thought bitterly.

She'd done it, then. Made him realise the truth. Her lip quivered. She pushed back the misery, determined to finish this before he hurt her any more. She sat up, feeling suddenly weak and defenceless.

'If you're trying to work out how to tell me you want to leave,' she said, in a brave attempt to sound indifferent, 'don't worry. Just pack and I think I'll get the message.'

His body had jerked when she'd spoken, as if he'd forgotten she was there. Hurt, Trish bullied her mouth into submission by jamming her teeth together, and it stopped trembling. The sooner they got this over the better.

'I don't want to leave,' he said abruptly.

Her heart faltered, recovered its beat and began to race. Relief swept over her, alarming her with its intensity. She waited without breathing, shaken by his flat, unemotional tone. He was telling her nothing. Did he want more sex or was he beginning to care? If he hadn't looked so dauntingly contained, she might have asked. Adam wasn't used to

150

sharing his private feelings. It would take time to know what went on in his head.

Why weren't men more expressive? They were supposed to be the uncomplicated ones. But they kept themselves tightly reined in, never giving anything away in case it might compromise them.

'You're shivering,' she said in a small voice.

Ruefully aware of her concern, that she loved and worried about him, she slid quickly from the bed, wrapping the sheet around her body. Then she unhooked the navy towelling robe from the door and handed it to him.

'Thanks.' He caught her hand and held it tightly but wouldn't look at her.

Here it comes, she thought bleakly. Her legs were trembling now, as she willed him to hurry through the brush-off routine so she could run to her room and give way to the threatening tears.

He was playing with her fingers, his beautiful eyes hidden by smoke-dark lids, as if he was trying to choose his words and let her down gently. She focused on the thick lashes marking twin black crescents on his high cheekbones and felt her heart lurch with helpless love.

'I can't believe I could have been so stupid!' he muttered under his breath.

Trish snatched her hand away. That was going too far! She opened her mouth indignantly to speak, then froze. He'd lifted his head and was gazing at her. And his molten dark eyes were spilling over with anger and pain.

All her instincts told her to take him in her arms and console him. Self-preservation dictated otherwise.

'I think you've just been offensive,' she snapped, and stalked back to bed where she sat in a taut right-angle, glaring at him defiantly.

He exhaled slowly as if he'd been storing up his breath for a long time. 'You don't understand. I've been blind, haven't I? Trish, I remember every curve and hollow of your body. It was imprinted on me. And it's different. You're...' Nervously she waited while he inhaled and then pushed all his words and breath out together in a harsh monotone. 'Pregnant.'

He began to pace the floor, glaring down at it. Disappointment lanced her heart like a sword. He didn't want her to be carrying his child. This was, after all, likely to be a short-term affair as far as he was concerned. A brief obsession which had no room for babies and nappies and a woman who'd become a mother instead of a lover. He wanted her to be his bed-mate, to amuse him, to devote herself to him exclusively. A baby would spoil all that for him, she thought miserably.

'If you are...' His mouth compressed as if he couldn't say the word, couldn't cope with what he'd done.

'Pregnant,' she supplied grimly.

'Are you?' When she nodded, he swayed and steadied himself by grasping the back of a chair. 'Our child,' he said hoarsely. He passed a shaky hand over his face.

'The beginning of a life,' she said, emotion threading her words with a trembling passion. Overwhelmed, she pressed both hands to her stomach and closed her eyes. Her baby would probably never know its father. Adam might send cheques regularly, but he clearly didn't want to be involved. His passion had cooled. Well. Better to know the truth, she thought.

Wanting to get rid of him before she broke down, she flung off the bedclothes and began hauling his clothes from the wardrobe, clutching at them blindly because of the tears in her eyes.

'Stop that!' he ordered.

'No!' she cried. 'You have to go! I love you and you don't care for me and it's destroying me, Adam!'

His case was on top of the wardrobe. Standing on tiptoe, she dragged it down—and found herself wrestling with Adam. They ended up on the floor with the case.

He covered her with his body. Kissed her hard. Held her by her wrists and drew them over her head so that she couldn't struggle. Soon she realised that her furious writhing was having an undesirable effect on them both. They were panting, snatching fast and desperate kisses as if they were about to part and never see one another again.

When he raised his mouth briefly, she lay rigid, hurting so much inside, she couldn't breathe or think. He kissed the tear stains all the way down her cheeks and across to the groove on her upper lip. Briefly his lips pressed to her eyes, warm and sweet, then he released her. She quickly rolled away and stood up.

'Trish.' He was there, with her, struggling with unknown emotions. 'You're jumping to the wrong conclusions. I am in deadly earnest about my feelings. I want you—'

'Sex!' she derided, challenging him to deny that.

'Yes!' His eyes burned like coals. 'My body goes haywire every time I see you—I've told you that! But I've also told you time and time again that I want you in other ways, that I do care deeply about you—'

'You never said "deeply"!' she cried, biting her lip in confusion.

'Deeply.' He kissed her. 'Deeply.' He kissed her again. 'Deeply.'

Mouths locked, they enjoyed the sweetness of each other's lips. Then Adam sighed. 'I've messed things up. I meant to take my time. Court you properly. I wanted us to become friends. But...you filled my mind, my heart, my soul,' he said huskily, tipping up her chin so that their eyes met. She trembled, awed by his passion, afraid of it. 'I had no idea that sex with the right person could be emotionally demanding. And I was stunned by my reactions when I realised you must be carrying our child.'

'What kind of stunned?' she asked doubtfully.

It took him a long time to answer. When he did, it was muttered so quietly that she barely heard. 'As in knocked sideways. Moved.' He shook his head helplessly. 'I—I felt a rush of feeling which—' He broke off and kissed her mouth tenderly. 'You must have been scared.'

He looked at her for a long time as if he didn't know what to say and she waited breathlessly for the words she wanted so badly to hear. 'No. I have people here who care for me,' she said eventually.

He frowned. 'Would you have kept it to yourself if I hadn't found out?'

'I don't know,' she replied honestly. 'If I'd thought you were playing around, yes, I suppose so. I didn't want you to feel a duty towards me. I still don't want that. I'm not sure of you, Adam,' she confessed. 'You're holding back so much of yourself—'

'I am what I am.'

He had spoken curtly, his face set in the expression she was coming to know: closed and determined and nearly—but not quite—hiding the pain in his eyes.

That expression haunted her. Because she loved him, she longed to root out its cause. One day she would. His passion would turn to love, she vowed. And he would let that ruthless restraint go.

She put her arms around his neck and laid her head on his chest. The thud of his heart pounded in her ear. She shifted her position and placed her hand there, lovingly.

'It's important to me that you should share your feelings.'

'I share what I can,' he said into the thick mass of her hair. 'I can do no more. You manage to love others unconditionally. Your grandmother must annoy you, but that doesn't make any difference. Christine was often irritable and short-tempered, but you let that wash over you and remained cheerful and loving. I've always admired you for not judging people, for concentrating on their good points. Can't you do that with me? I want our relationship to grow. We have a child to think of, our baby.'

'Our baby!' she echoed, her face shining with happiness.

'Take me as I am, Trish.'

'Warts and all?'

'You've noticed!' he cried in mock horror.

The tension had been broken, the sticking point glossed over. For the moment, she would be content. He was giving her as much of himself as he could and speaking of a long-term future. But was he sacrificing too much? What of his love of city life, excitement, glamour and sophistication?

'You have a lot to lose by staying with me,' she said soberly.

'Stress, high blood pressure, an early heart attack—!'

'No, idiot!' She smiled up at him, then became serious again. 'You're doing all the surrendering, Adam—'

'I'm taking. Walking away from a life which would probably kill me before I'm sixty. It's only when you stop running, Trish, that you discover how pleasant it is to walk.' His arms tightened around her. 'I'm not denying that it'll be a culture shock, or that it won't be easy. I've hardly been here five minutes. But the magic has already sunk into my bones. When I left, I felt bereft. Maybe because I was leaving you, but I believe it was more than that. Otherwise why would I feel a sense of calm and delight the minute I looked out of the helicopter window and saw the islands in the distance?'

'I want desperately to believe you—'

'And I desperately want it to work. So between us,' he said with a grin, 'it should!'

Her face showed her lingering doubts. 'And your business?'

'No problem there. I can be on the mainland in a very short time if necessary. Most of the time I can easily run it from here.'

'Where?' She pulled away, her eyes concerned. 'I'll need your room soon—and I'm full up for the rest of the season! There's nowhere for you to go—'

'I'll find somewhere, don't worry. Leave that to me.'

'I do worry,' she said, frowning. 'About your taking these huge decisions to change your life—'

'I'm more concerned about you. If we stay together, the age difference will show up more and more. You've spent half your life looking after other people. Do you really want to add a crotchety old man to your repertoire?'

'If it's you, yes,' she said, her face suffused with joy at the thought of being with Adam until they were old and decrepit! 'But you wouldn't be crotchety. I'd make you laugh.'

'I think you might!' he agreed with a chuckle. 'Is it really that simple, this problem of our ages?'

'It's the least of our problems,' she replied, her expression grave.

'Do you love me?' he asked in a low tone.

'Totally,' she replied, gazing at him with a ravenous hunger.

His mouth touched hers in a sweet, breathtakingly tender kiss. 'Then that's all I need to know, Trish. Everything else is a mere detail.' He took her hand and kissed it passionately. Then, trailing a forefinger along her collar-bone, he said more throatily, 'I'm going to take a shower. Join me, mermaid. I'll show you how committed I am.'

Afterwards, while he was in the middle of drying her, he held her tightly, rained kisses on her face and then demanded breakfast.

'Am I allowed to dress first?' she asked with mock indignation.

His hot gaze made her bones dissolve in a moment. 'My ultimate fantasy!' he murmured with a lecherous leer. 'Being served bacon and eggs by a nude goddess—'

'Well, fancy that! We have something in common,' she declared, her hands jauntily planted on the swell of her hips. 'My fantasy is the same. But substitute nude god.'

'I fear the bacon fat might cause problems in the god's lower regions,' Adam said drily.

She giggled. 'I'll get dressed—'

He caught her hand. 'Trish...' Nervous excitement rippled through her body. He was going to say it. The words she longed to hear were on his lips, waiting, ready... He cleared his throat. She held her breath. 'Two eggs, three rashers?' he suggested.

'Coward,' she said fondly. He looked shocked, confirming her suspicion that he'd chickened out, and she smiled. Pleased with herself for interpreting his intention so well, she detached her hand and went to find some clothes.

A new confidence settled within her. For the first time she dared to hope for the future. She began to hum happily to herself as she pulled on her jeans. Our baby, she thought fondly, planning a shopping spree for maternity clothes. And she'd tell her grandmother, Lucy, Joe—oh, everyone!

A few moments later, Adam appeared in her bedroom doorway, dressed already in a pair of jeans and a beautifully tight-fitting T-shirt. 'Or, on second thoughts, one egg, two sausages—'

She threw her hairbrush at him. 'Get the ingredients ready!' she said with a grin, wrapping a towel around her wet hair. 'I'll be thirty seconds. You be ready or I'll serve your breakfast down the front of your jeans!'

Adam laughed and wandered down the stairs. Slipping her feet into her old plimsolls, she followed, loving the way he played stupid as she barked out orders. And she found herself dissolving into giggles at his obsequious bowing and scraping.

'Oh, please don't!' she gasped, weak with laughter after a truly nauseating display of cringing. 'I think I prefer Valentino Capelli!'

'Ah!' he cried, leaping into the part at once and bending her back with theatrical skill.

'That's the wrong Valentino,' she gasped. 'You're copying Rudolph!'

'Is good, no? My woman, she getting hot, eh?'

'Your woman, she getting backache,' she told him tartly. 'And hungry. For *breakfast*!' she added.

'Damn!' he said with easygoing disappointment, bringing her to the vertical again. 'OK. We eat. Shall I be Mother?'

'Just pour the tea,' she replied, her eyes scathing. But she was smiling. And overjoyed. They ate, they argued, they laughed. It seemed that the past four years had never happened. Yet there was a difference. Adam was now her lover and the father of her baby.

'I'm crazy about the way you are,' he said, leaning over to kiss her across the table.

'Chewing a sausage, with egg on my chin?' she hazarded.

'Fresh and unadorned—'

'Great gorges of wrinkles—'

'Laughter lines,' he corrected her, 'but only if I get very close and go cross-eyed.'

'Ruddy-faced—'

'Don't swear,' he reproved. 'Scrubbed and pink.'

He abandoned his breakfast and came over to kiss as much scrubbed and pink as he could get to, before she pushed him away with a growled, 'Oh, let a girl eat her grub in peace!'

'Some women,' he said huffily, being Mother again and pouring more tea, 'have no idea of romance.'

'Don't go to London tomorrow!' she said suddenly, catching his hand.

'I don't want to, but…I must,' he answered. He hesitated. 'Trish, I'll need to do some work on my computer today. Don't mind if I shut myself in my room, do you?'

'Yes,' she said honestly, making him smile.

But he worked all day and she didn't see him—apart from when she took in cups of coffee and sandwiches—until the evening.

'Dinner's ready,' she finally said tentatively, popping her head around his door. He'd been staring at the monitor, his arms folded, and she wondered how much work he had done. And what he'd been thinking about.

That night they made love and she fell asleep in his arms. It was hard for her when they said their goodbyes the next morning at Anneka's Quay because of the low tide. She clung to him, trying not to show how upset she felt, trying to be cheerful and to trust him to come back. But he sussed her out.

'I'll return in a couple of days. I'll ring you every evening and every morning. Watch you don't bump into something on your way home,' he said fondly. 'Your eyes are all misted over. You need windscreen wipers.'

She laughed ruefully, and then he had pushed her away

and was striding onto the boat. Although it was a blur, she waved at it frantically till she was all alone on the quay and she had no choice but to turn and make her way home.

The loneliness hit her like a wall. Silence where there had been laughter. She went up to his room and snuggled her face into the soft cashmere jumper he'd left on a chair.

Nothing must come between them. This was the love of her life. Without him, everything would be meaningless. Gently she replaced the jumper and went downstairs, intending to do some jobs, but she couldn't settle.

On an impulse, she rang Petra on the chance that she was off duty from the hospital where she worked as a staff nurse. Perhaps she could throw some light on Adam's refusal to abandon himself to his emotions.

'I gave your love to Mr Mack Rowe,' she announced tartly, when Petra answered.

'Jolly good,' said Petra encouragingly.

'You rat! Where's your apology? You knew it was Adam!'

'Who am I to stop a lovely romance?'

Trish's eyes widened. 'What is this? Bush telegraph?'

'Oh, for goodness' sake!' Petra groaned. 'It's hardly the biggest secret in the world! He loves you—'

'What makes you think that?' Trish cried in amazement, her heart rate beginning to endanger her health. 'Have you been talking to him? What have you said? What did he say?'

'Look, you dim-witted yokel,' her friend said affectionately, 'of course he loves you! A child of two could tell that with a blindfold on and earplugs the size of pillows. He's been nuts about you ever since you fetched up on our doorstep! I knew that, Mother knew—even Stephen knew! Why do you think Stevie gave you hell? He was scared witless that you'd become his wicked stepmother!'

'Petra, stop making things up!' said Trish in exasperation. 'He hasn't said—'

'Well, he wouldn't, would he? Adam keeps a respectful distance where emotions are concerned,' Petra said gently.

'He's always avoided anything that might hurt him. He didn't go to Mother's funeral, if you remember.'

Something he'd said came to the forefront of her mind. Trish hesitated, then asked, 'Pets, why would he have married Christine? He told me he didn't love her—but that he'd needed someone. What do you make of that?'

'Sounds like a teenager trying to escape his family or something. Abusive father. Drunken mother, family drug ring...' she said, going over the top as usual. 'I don't know! I was three at the time! He never talked...Trish, this is odd...he never talked about his family! Not a word. Listen, duckie, it's not anything to do with you. He loves you and that's that. OK? Got that in your peasant brain?'

Trish caught herself grinning idiotically. 'I hope you're right, darling!' she cried fervently.

'Course I am! Now, how's your gran?'

'Fine, apart from complaining of a broken heart because none of the doctors will marry her and demanding they find some superglue for it!' She giggled. Everyone in the hospital had adored her grandmother. 'She's going to stay with a friend on St Mary's to recuperate, so she can be near the hospital.'

Trish didn't speak her private thoughts. Judging by the way her grandmother had announced this with a suspiciously overacted casualness, it was a ploy to leave the scene clear for her romance with Adam to develop!

She and Petra chatted for a little while and then Trish rang off. Hugging herself, she danced around the kitchen. He loved her! She had no doubt of that now.

Two days later she was jumping up and down on the quay in agitation, willing the boat to hurry up. 'Adam!' she yelled excitedly, seeing him standing in the bow. 'Adam!'

He waved, a broad grin lighting his face. He was first to leap off the boat, holding out his arms, and she ran into them, overjoyed to see him.

They held one another for so long without moving that all the passengers had disembarked and the boat had moved away before they parted. Ridiculously happy, she lifted her face for his kiss.

'I've missed you so much!' she said fervently.

'I've missed you too. How are you?'

'We're fine,' she answered tenderly.

He kissed her again, as if bemused. 'The traffic was awful. Terrible stink of petrol fumes and you wouldn't believe the noise—I couldn't sleep. What are you laughing at?' he demanded.

'You!' she cried in delight, her eyes dancing. 'You sound like a true islander!'

Looking around him wearily, he passed a hand over his forehead and pressed his fingers to his temples. 'It is good to be back. I have a foul headache. Stephen gave me some pills but I've run out.'

'I'll find you something, darling,' she said sympathetically. 'Let's get you back. The walk will help you to unwind. How was Stephen?'

'We had a row,' he admitted as they trudged up the path. 'I was already irritable and wishing I was with you and not mopping up the chaos I found at the office. Louise has apparently disappeared with some viscount and hasn't been seen for two days. She left a message saying she wants me to buy her out. Stephen came in at a bad moment and I lost my temper with him.'

'You must ring him up and smooth things over,' she said soothingly.

'I have other priorities. I need to organise my business so that I can work from here. I have some computer equipment coming, and office furniture. Once that's arrived, I can be in touch with everyone and keep tabs on what's going on.'

Trish reached up and smoothed the worry lines on his forehead. 'Is that wise?' she asked anxiously. 'You're sure you want to commit yourself—'

'I am committed,' he said tersely. 'I'll prove that to you.'

Trish found him a homoeopathic remedy for his headache when they reached her cottage and he took it—mainly to please her.

'How's Lucy?' he asked casually, when he'd taken his case upstairs.

'Missing your lessons!' she said with a wry grimace.

He gave a nervous smile and quickly averted his gaze, as if he was anxious not to make her jealous. 'I'll try to fit in extra. How about showing me round the island properly?' he suggested. 'After that demonstration of affection at the quayside just now, I imagine all the inhabitants know what colour my toothbrush is by now!'

Trish groaned and rolled her eyes. 'They'll know far more than that! I hope you don't mind being discussed. Everyone'll be agog to meet you. Come on. Let's see how many people happen to walk out of their front doors the minute we happen by!'

She was pleasantly surprised to see how well Adam got on with Joe Slater and his wife. So well, in fact, that Joe offered to let Adam use one wing of the large farmhouse for accommodation and an office. The two men wandered off deep in conversation, leaving Trish and Dot Slater to talk about the lack of offers for the leasehold.

'Can't keep the farm on,' Dot said. 'We'm too old. It'll go to rack and ruin without proper attention. We got the bungalow ready, on St Mary's, but don't want to move till this place is sorted out. We owe it to Ned to see he don't lose his job.'

Trish covered Dot's hand with hers. Lucy's brother had been very worried about the situation. 'Something'll turn up,' she said reassuringly. Her eyes were wistful when she looked around the big farmhouse kitchen. 'I've always loved it here. I'd buy it like a shot if I won the lottery.'

'Too late!' Adam and Joe had walked in, both of them looking extraordinarily pleased with themselves. 'I've bought it,' said Adam, with a casualness that didn't match his excited face.

'You?' cried Trish in astonishment. 'But why? You're not a farmer! Adam, are you mad?'

'Probably,' he said, grinning at her. His whole face was suffused with delight at the women's amazement. 'I mean to run my business from here. Ned can work the land. Don't you think it's a brilliant solution?'

'Oh, Adam!' she cried, running over to fling her arms around him. 'That's wonderful! Ned and Lucy will be so relieved!'

'And you,' he said, smiling down at her. 'What do you think of having me for a neighbour?'

She sighed happily. It meant more to her than he'd ever know. This was a very solid commitment. Her expression told him what she felt, but mischievously she said, 'Wonderful! I'll be able to borrow the ATV whenever I like!'

'Materialistic female,' he muttered. But he laughed at her fondly and hugged her till she was breathless.

'Joe, get out the home-made wine. The dandelion and burdock we made last year,' ordered Dot excitedly, bustling off to get some glasses. 'This calls for a celebration. Don't suppose you've got a brother, have you?' she asked Adam with a grin, as he and Trish separated and came to the table.

Adam's smile was wiped from his face in an instant. In the act of sitting down, he stared at her bleakly for a split second, and then eased himself into the chair and said, quite normally, 'No. I haven't. Why?' But Trish had seen his distress. She knew now that it was something to do with his family.

'Well,' said Dot, quite unaware of how tightly Adam's fists were clenched, 'Lucy could do with a nice chap like you.'

'She'll find someone,' he said confidently. With great care, he uncurled his fists and laid his palms on his knees. 'She's a cracker.'

'Thinks the world of you,' observed Dot.

'Yes, well,' he said, looking uncomfortable.

Trish frowned, wondering why. A nasty little doubt crept into her mind and she pushed it away. Adam wouldn't go to such lengths to prove he was planning a future with her if he was playing around with Lucy on the side. It would work, she told herself, feeling a gentle warmth steal over her as she watched the men eagerly discussing arrangements, and Dot, seeing the blind love in Trish's eyes, took her hand, squeezed it and gave her a fond, understanding smile.

After a while, Trish and Adam left. They walked hand in hand around Samson Hill while she told him some of the old stories about shipwrecks and smuggling. The Tresco Flats spread out before them, gleaming stretches of sand crowded with gulls. Elegant terns dived for sand eels in the crystal-clear water, then soared into the clear blue sky again in joyous flight.

She heaved a huge sigh of happiness. She could tell from Adam's face that he loved the wild beauty as much as she did.

Her arm slipped around his waist. 'I want to show you something,' she said quietly. 'Come to the church. I think you ought to meet Grandpa. Gran and I often go to his grave and talk to him.'

He stiffened imperceptibly. 'No... I... Trish, I think I'd better get back and make some phone calls to my solicitor—'

'All of a sudden?' she asked, watching tension draw his mouth into a hard line. *Give in to it!* she pleaded silently. Stop fighting with your boots on!

He attempted a bright smile which didn't quite work. 'I've just made the deal of my life!' he declared. 'I ought to start the ball rolling.'

'That's not the reason you want to duck out of my invitation,' she persisted. 'It's about your brother, isn't it?'

'Did I say I had a brother?' he shot at her warily.

'No,' she replied, 'but I think you had one and he died. And that's what you've shut away—'

'Then that's where I want to leave him.'

Trish assessed his mood. Grim, she decided. Unbending.

'Your choice,' she said sadly.

The episode deflated her high spirits. She tried to lighten the atmosphere by asking him about his plans for the farm, and soon they were talking with apparent friendliness again. But there was a barrier between them. And it worried her.

May became June. Wild flowers carpeted the islands. The summer heat filled the air with perfume and bees, and the boats—and Trish's guesthouse—were filled with tourists. Despite working long hours, she and Adam managed to spend all their spare time together, enjoying each other's company more than she could have imagined.

Her grandmother returned, having triumphantly bought more cherries and cabbage roses for her wedding hat, and Trish told her about the baby, wanting her to be the first to know.

Casually her grandmother dipped into her capacious bag of knitting and brought out some psychedelic matinée jackets and bootees.

'You...*knew*!' gasped Trish, her eyes rounding.

'Probably before you did, duck. Now, why aren't you two sleeping together?'

'I'm not sure of him,' Trish replied, a little shocked by such directness.

'Make him sure,' her grandmother told her, and picked up her knitting again.

So Trish took that advice and moved in with Adam, commuting between the two houses. Their lovemaking became more intense. Sometimes sweet and tender, sometimes urgent and frantic. But always profoundly earth-shattering, and her love for him grew deeper every day. She couldn't believe she could be so happy—or that they were so perfectly matched. There were times when he laughed her into bed—and those were the most joyous times of all.

Everyone liked him. Lucy especially. She followed him around with adoring eyes and would have made Trish jealous if she hadn't been assured every day and night of Adam's wholehearted affection.

Returning from seeing her friends at Fraggle Rock Café one afternoon, she reflected that Adam had adapted surprisingly well. He hadn't been to the mainland once. She

admired him for his single-minded determination to partici-
pate fully in island life.

Lucy's brother, Ned, often took him out in Joe's old boat
which Adam had bought. Ned was teaching him the safe
passages around the islands and patiently explaining the
differing sea and tide conditions. After each trip, Adam
would come back full of enthusiasm, eager to tell her where
he'd been and what birds or seals they'd seen.

Books about the Scillies and birdlife lay in heaps on the
tables in the farmhouse sitting room and he pored over
them at every opportunity. He was the most passionate man
she'd ever known, and his love of life and learning everything about his environment made him very dear to her.

She and Adam sometimes worked on the farm with Ned,
or spent happy hours decorating one of the many rooms. It
seemed they had everything they wanted. Occasionally, in
the quiet hush before dawn, she would lie awake, wondering if such profound happiness could last for ever. Then
Adam would wake, kiss her lovingly and she believed that
it really would.

Lucy adored her computer lessons. Adam said she was
a natural. In fact, Trish decided, pushing open the front
door of her cottage, they'd be working right now. Perhaps
she'd take them a slice of 'Death by Chocolate' and some
home-made lemonade.

Singing contentedly to herself, she made up a tray and
carried it carefully next door. She was about to go into
Adam's study when she heard an odd sound. A frown drew
her brows together. It sounded like someone breathing
heavily. She listened more intently. *Adam?* And now…
Lucy?

Slowly she placed the tray on a nearby table, her heart
thudding like a steam hammer in her chest. As white as a
sheet, she listened again. They couldn't be. He wouldn't…
Her mind raced. He thought Lucy was beautiful. Had great
legs. Lucy adored him. But surely…

She gulped, despair tugging at her heart as she remembered the first time she'd been suspicious of him, and how

he'd put her mind at rest. Afraid of what she might see, she picked up the tray to take away again. The tumblers slid and clinked against one another because her hands were trembling so much.

And then, to her utter dismay, the study door opened.

CHAPTER EIGHT

'DARLING! I thought I heard you!' said Adam enthusiastically.

Trish searched his face for signs of guilt. He looked flushed, but his eyes were affectionate and warm. 'I—I didn't know whether to disturb you—'

'Idiot,' he said fondly, taking the tray and carrying it into the room. 'Disturb me any time with cake! Lucy! Look what Trish has brought to keep us going!'

'I'll leave you to it,' Trish mumbled.

She felt ashamed for doubting him. Then her eyes fell on Lucy. She looked like a rabbit caught in torchlight, her hair tumbled about as if... *No!* Trish thought in horror. She felt as if she'd been punched in the solar plexus. Nausea rose in hot waves, making her head swim. Not Adam and Lucy. Please no...

'If you're sure you won't stay...' Adam said, positioning himself near the door.

He seemed anxious to get rid of her. She bit her lip.

'Lots to do,' she choked.

'Are you all right, darling?' he asked gently.

Trish clapped a hand over her mouth and raced for the downstairs cloakroom where she was violently sick. Exhausted, she cleaned herself up, staring at her white, miserable face in the mirror like a zombie.

Adam was waiting outside and he immediately took her in his arms. Limp and bewildered, she let him lead her up to their bedroom and tuck her shivering body beneath the duvet.

'You're very hot,' he said anxiously, feeling her forehead. 'Probably a bug you've picked up. I'll get the doctor—'

'No, Adam,' she said in a monotone. 'You only call the

doctor out in a dire emergency. If it's a bug, I can treat it—'

'You need proper medicine—'

'It *is* proper medicine!' she exploded. 'I won't take drugs! Don't you belittle my beliefs! Didn't your headache go away shortly after I treated you? Didn't Gran's arm heal faster than the doctors could have believed? I won't have you thrusting your toxic drugs on me, especially now. Do you want to kill your child? Is that what you're after?'

'Trish! Don't talk like that!' He looked shocked by her hysterical outburst. 'I'm sorry. Of course you have a right to your beliefs. I was only worried about you. You look a peculiar colour. I don't want anything to happen to you—'

'Leave me alone!'

'Do you have a headache?' he asked. 'Is the light bothering you?'

'No. But I want to sleep,' she muttered irritably. She turned her head away.

She felt his mouth on her cheek, heard his murmured, 'I'll check on you later. You'll be all right?' She nodded and then the door closed.

She didn't know what to think. Maybe her imagination was going into overdrive. Adam had given up a great deal for her, after all. Angrily, she pummelled the pillow into a more comfortable shape and curled up, feeling self-pity for the first time in her life.

Lucy had old-fashioned values. Maybe she'd just felt embarrassed at being alone with Trish's lover. Almost anything made Lucy blush. Though that didn't explain the heavy breathing…unless they'd been struggling to move a desk, or scrabbling under the computer station to unplug things, she thought vaguely. There must be an explanation. Adam wouldn't two-time her. Surely?

Her fears were mounting by the minute and she knew she had to voice them or she would go mad. The thought of his infidelity was eating into her and making her feel more and more nauseous.

She bit her lip hard, terrified that he'd prove to be a

compulsive womaniser. Now she felt really sick. For the
sake of her baby she had to calm down. Feeling weak and
forlorn, she got up and went to her own cottage to take
some Rescue Remedy. When she felt a little stronger, she'd
find him and...

It was then that she heard him. A low laugh. A
gasp...from Lucy. They were here, in her cottage! Her
mind whirled. Had they come straight here, after she'd
driven them out? she thought wildly. Had Adam imagined
that they'd be safe here?

Shaking like a leaf, she climbed the stairs and slowly
turned the handle of her bedroom door. Before it had
opened more than an inch or two, her hand faltered and she
stood rooted to the spot, appalled by what she was seeing.

Adam. Not where he was supposed to be. Not in any
way. His back was to her. Lucy was in his arms—virtually
hidden from view, but Trish recognised her shoes and her
voice.

'Oh, Adam!' Lucy cried passionately. 'This is wonderful!'

In a state of utter shock, Trish closed the door and
walked away. Staggered down the stairs blindly. Fell over
a chair. Began to weep as she fumbled her way to the back
door and stumbled off to a hidden corner, far away in the
farmhouse garden, where she crumpled in a small, miserable heap, crying her heart out.

And then she realised she was going to be sick again.
Weeping with distress, she made it to the cloakroom just
in time.

'Trish! Trish, you there?'

Too weak to hide from Adam, she feebly washed her
face, gave it a perfunctory dab with a towel and waited for
him to come in, because she couldn't move.

'We thought we heard you downstairs in the cottage. I've
been looking for you everywhere. Still sick, sweetheart?'
he asked sympathetically.

She nodded. Reached out a hand because, much as she

loathed him, she needed help. 'Get me to bed,' she muttered
rawly.

'You've been crying! Darling—'

'No, Adam. Don't fuss. Don't "darling" me. Just get—
me—in—to—bed!' she said jerkily.

With great care, he helped her to the bedroom and guided
her to the bed. His fingers began to fiddle with the buttons
of her shirt. She drew back, her eyes huge and accusing.

'What is it?' he asked gently. 'Does that hurt?'

'Yes!' she wailed. 'It all hurts!' Overcome with grief,
she bundled herself into bed, fully dressed, and lay with
her back to him.

'I'm worried about you. There could be something wrong
with the baby. You have to let me get the doctor,' he said
sternly.

She heard him lifting the phone from the hook. 'Leave
it!' she yelled, whipping around, her hair tumbling over her
tear-stained face.

'God, Trish!' he said in exasperation. 'I don't know
what's come over you! You're fevered. You don't know
what you're doing!'

She did. She was disintegrating, bit by bit. Staring at
him, loving, hating him, she felt her emotions overwhelming her again. Sobs racked her body and she fell back on
the pillow as torrents of tears flowed down her face, salting
her parched lips.

'Go away!' she sobbed.

'No. I couldn't leave you.'

He gathered her up, ignoring her feeble struggles, and he
held her, stroking her hair, occasionally kissing her forehead or mopping up her tears with his handkerchief. Too
distraught to fight with him, she pretended he wasn't there.

Because soon that was how it would be.

What hurt her most was that Lucy had spoken without
stammering. Adam had relaxed Lucy so perfectly with his
skilled brand of sweet-talk and lies and lovemaking, she
thought bitterly, that Lucy had spoken clearly for the first
time in her life.

Did he mean to keep them both satisfied? She tormented herself with that thought, and then wondered what would happen to Lucy if Adam tired of her. The girl was so fragile, so sensitive, that it would leave her in a terrible mess. How could he risk the emotions of *two* women? she raged, weeping uncontrollably.

'Please, Trish, please stop!' he pleaded harshly in her ear, shaking her in his anxiety. 'I'll need to go and tell Lucy to look after your guests—'

'Yes! Go!' she snuffled. A huge sob tore through her and she feared for her baby. 'Go,' she repeated, desperately controlling her tears. 'I want to sleep.'

'I'll be back,' he promised.

But she said nothing and turned to face the wall.

Hours, a day, another and then another came and went in a blur of tears and torture. In her mind, she went through all the signs she'd ignored. His undisguised attraction to Lucy. The supposed 'computer lessons'. He'd deceived her whilst pretending to be Mr Wonderful, promising her total commitment, going through all the right motions. For that, she'd never forgive him.

Thankfully the sickness had stabilised but she felt lethargic and uninterested. Adam tried to talk to her but she pushed him away, and when he offered to get her grandmother she yelled at him like a fishwife.

'I'm sorry!' she mumbled, shamefaced. There was no reason for her to descend to his level. 'I don't want Gran to be worried. Tell her it might be catching and I won't let her near me.'

Looking hollow-eyed, he nodded. Cynically she wondered if he was finding it hard, managing a harem. How often had he crept off to see Lucy? Burning the candle at both ends didn't suit him, she thought sourly. And thinking of him and Lucy perhaps making love on the camomile turf together made her burst into floods of tears.

'Trish, you can't go on like this! Think of your baby! You need help. I have someone downstairs waiting to see you,' Adam said gently.

'Not Lucy!' she muttered in dismay.

He brushed back the hair from her hot, damp forehead, smiled and left the room. She vowed that if he'd brought a doctor she'd hurl the bedside lamp at him. Scowling from beneath her lowered brows, she waited to see who it was. When the handsome young man appeared with Adam, she opened her mouth in astonishment.

'Stephen!' she cried weakly.

'Hi. Sorry to hear you're not well,' he said, with suspicious interest. 'I came over to see Dad. Got a few days off,' he explained, sitting on the bed. He put a briefcase on the floor and rummaged around in it. 'What have you taken for this virus?' he asked, suddenly brisk and professional. 'I've got a couple of things here...'

Trish's eyes narrowed. 'This isn't a casual visit, so don't pretend it is!' She drew in a sharp breath. 'You asked him here, didn't you?' she snapped at Adam.

He frowned. 'What if I did? Let him help you. He's got something to calm you down—'

'How *dare* you? He's not even qualified! And you know my views—'

'I didn't know what to do,' he said tightly. 'I know nothing of your remedies. You didn't want a local doctor and you asked me not to tell your grandmother—what was I supposed to do? Watch you get sicker and sicker?'

'I'm not sick any more.' She glowered.

'No. Just behaving bizarrely,' he replied, grim-lipped.

Sparks were flying between them. The air seemed charged with their emotions. He was angry with *her*! How dared he be?

'It was utterly high-handed of you to drag Stephen over here, all this way—!' she began furiously.

'I'd have abducted the Prime Minister if I'd thought it might do any good!' he growled.

'You're not my keeper!' she yelled. 'You don't have any rights over me! My body's mine, do you hear? I don't want anything to do with you.'

She stopped her tirade, shocked by Adam's white face.

Colour had drained from it completely and he was swaying. Stephen, looking concerned, steadied his father and there passed between them a look of affection, which touched her heart.

'She's ill. She doesn't mean it,' Stephen said gently.

'I do!' she cried, incensed to be patronised like a silly child. 'I don't want to be involved with you, Adam. It's very simple.'

He'd withdrawn into that private fortress where he kept his emotions safely chained up. Totally in control, he asked coldly, 'Why?'

She flung him a look of scorn. 'Work it out for yourself!'

'I'm sorry, Stephen,' Adam said curtly. 'I brought you here to no avail. Thanks for coming. I appreciate it.'

'Not often you say you need me,' Stephen said drily. The two men once again exchanged looks of mutual sympathy.

Unable to bear any more, Trish slid from the bed, grabbed her clothes and headed for the *en suite* bathroom.

'What are you up to?' Adam demanded menacingly.

She whirled round, her face riven with anger. 'I'm dressing and I'm going back to my cottage. *If* you've finished with it, that is!'

As she stalked to the bathroom door, she heard Stephen's voice.

'She's off her rocker, if you ask me...'

The rest of his sentence was lost and she realised the men must have left the bedroom and gone downstairs.

'Good!' she muttered viciously, pulling on her clothes haphazardly, with little regard for the strength of the fabric or her own tortured body beneath.

She looked ghastly. Running her fingers through her hair, she wished for some foundation to mask her blotchiness and give her some colour instead of the Morticia-like whiteness, which made her eyes look so dark and haunted. Then she gave a wry smile at her stupidity. What did it matter how dreary she looked? She could shave her head and grow a moustache and it wouldn't make any difference.

The men were in the kitchen. 'I want a word with you,' she said coldly to Adam.

'Mutual,' he growled. 'Outside.' He strode alongside her till they came to where the farmland met the little beach. They stopped, an angry two yards apart. 'Well?' he asked in a threatening tone.

'No, it's not *well*!' she cried, flipping up her chin in a stubborn, aggressive gesture. 'Don't you ever use my house or my bedroom for your vile deeds again!' she fumed.

'What vile deeds might those be?' he demanded.

'Oh! We're going to get a denial now, are we? Even though I saw you with my own eyes! You and your London ways and morals! Don't you know that over here it's not *done* to play fast and loose with secret lovers and—?'

'What the hell are you talking about, Trish?' he scathed, his eyes black with anger. 'London doesn't have exclusive rights on immorality, any more than the Islands are exclusively decent. I'm not playing fast—'

'I saw you!' she stormed. 'You liar!'

'Ridiculous! That's impossible. It must have been someone else!'

She stared in amazement. He sounded totally convincing! 'I don't believe this! I catch you making love to Lucy—'

'*Lucy?* Don't be ridiculous! What is this? Are you trying to break up our relationship?'

'I don't have to,' she muttered, her glare ferocious. 'You already did!'

'If you want to reject me for reasons of your own,' he said, incredibly contained, tense in every muscle and clearly simmering with an explosive rage as he spat out each word, 'then have the decency to say so. Don't invent lies that accuse me and someone else of immoral actions—'

'I walked in on you! In my bedroom! You and Lucy, panting for one another, and she telling you how wonderful it all was, *talking* to you as if she'd never known what it was like to stutter—!'

'Damn you, Trish!' he roared. He grabbed her arm. 'You

trust me that little? Stop struggling! I don't want to hurt you or the baby, but you'll come with me!'

'Where?' she wailed as he half-dragged, half-frogmarched her along.

'To see Lucy,' he snarled. 'There's something she and I have to tell you.'

'No! *No!*' she wept, her imagination rocketing into overdrive. 'Adam, don't do this to me! If you and she love one another, then I couldn't bear to hear—'

'For God's sake, Trish, shut up!' he hissed.

She began to cry. He ignored her. She'd never seen him so angry and she felt very scared. He and Lucy would announce their love for one another and she would have to stand there and take it. Beautiful Lucy, made whole by the man she loved. Adam...tender, passionate, irresistible, living with Lucy in the farmhouse. Next door. While she brought up her baby alone.

A primal moan burst from her throat as her legs buckled. Adam gave a rough curse and picked her up, then powered his way angrily to the cottage. Terrified, Trish stared at his impassive face and glittering black eyes and shrank at his ruthlessness. He would ride roughshod over anyone to do what he wanted, get what he wanted, she thought. She cursed the day they ever became lovers.

Adam had never felt so angry. None too gently, he set Trish down and pushed her towards a chair where she sat like a rag doll, her face tear-streaked and utterly miserable.

Damn her!

'Lucy!' he roared.

Wide-eyed and startled, Lucy came hurrying in, a load of sheets for washing in her hands. Impatiently, he snatched them from her.

'Wh-wh-wh—?' Lucy looked upset, her eyes flicking nervously from his seething face to Trish's.

Stephen came in, looking at the tense group for some kind of explanation. They ignored him.

'We're going to tell Trish what we've been doing these

past few weeks,' he said, reining in his anger for Lucy's sake.

She smiled at him in delight. He went to her, turned her so that she was sideways on to Trish. Lucy gazed blissfully into his eyes and he was aware of a choking sound from where Trish sat, but he refused to pay her any attention.

Placing his hands on Lucy's diaphragm, he smiled encouragingly into her eyes and said softly, 'Say it. Don't be afraid. You'll be fine.'

'Dad!' cried Stephen in shock. Adam silenced him with a look.

Lucy's eyes sparkled with happiness. She drew in a deep breath, expanding his splayed fingers. And in an outrush of breath said, 'My name is Lucy Ward.' Another look of delight, another breath. 'I live with my brother on Bryher.'

Adam beamed with triumph and kissed Lucy on both cheeks. 'Well done.' He turned to Trish, to see her reaction.

She was crying. 'You love her!' she sobbed. 'No—it's all right, Lucy!' she said, defending herself from Lucy's gasp of dismay. 'I'm not stupid enough to pursue someone who doesn't love me. I'm pleased for you—'

'You don't get it, do you?' he said in exasperation. 'Tell her, Lucy. Explain in simple, one-syllable words. On your own. Without me this time.'

Lucy inhaled. He could see the misery in her eyes and wondered if she'd fail. He held his breath too.

'Adam's been teaching me to breathe.' Pause. Good girl, he thought. 'We were keeping it a secret from you.' Her hand fluttered on her ribcage and then came away as she gained confidence. His heart softened for her. She'd done it! 'We wanted to give you a surprise on your birthday. To show you how well I'd done. I've been to St Mary's. Talking to strangers.' A huge grin split her face. 'Strangers!' she squealed. 'And...Adam doesn't love me! He—'

'That's brilliant, Lucy,' he said quickly. 'Well, Trish, I think you owe Lucy an apology.'

'I saw you both,' she said stubbornly. 'Heard you panting—'

'Breathing,' he snapped. 'I was teaching her to breathe! You couldn't have seen us making love. It never happened. All I've ever done is to put my hands on her diaphragm as you saw just now and make her inhale and push all the air out of her lungs—and with it any nervous tension. You have to believe that, for Lucy's sake. I don't care what you think of me, but she's very fond of you and likes working for you. So get it into your thick head: Lucy and I are not lovers, never have been and never will be, lovely though she is!'

'You must believe him,' Lucy said gently, her sweet face full of concern, and he saw the truth dawn on Trish's face.

'I've done it again, haven't I?' she mumbled. 'I saw and heard things and thought... Forgive me. I—I'm thrilled you're speaking so well, Lucy. You must be over the moon. Thank you, Adam,' she added stiffly. 'You will have changed her life and neither of us will ever forget that.'

Something inside him twisted, making him wince. He watched Trish and Lucy hug one another without much sense of joy himself. Saw Stephen's eyes on the women, how his son's gaze lingered on Lucy's affectionate face.

Trish turned to him, her eyes wet with tears. 'Adam—' she began brokenly.

Suddenly he couldn't stay. He made a dismissive gesture with his hand and exited abruptly.

She caught him up on the treacherous cliffs above Hell Bay. There must have been a storm at sea because the rollers were frighteningly high, roaring into the bay like steam trains.

He watched her running up the steep, peaty black path, clutching her side as if she had a stitch. And still she continued, dogged and determined to the last. Briefly he worried about her, about the child she carried. His child. Then that was too much of a torture and he shut his thoughts away, hurrying instead towards her so that she stopped trying to break her neck as she stumbled hysterically along.

'I think we've said all we have to say,' he told her, coldly and clinically, while she was trying to catch her breath.

'I've—apologised! Do you want—to punish me?'

His mouth curled in contempt. 'You talked of trust, once. Was your trust in me so weak that you'd jump to the wrong conclusions about me every time our relationship was challenged? What hope does that give us for the future?'

She stared at him in abject misery. 'How could I trust you,' she said, her voice shaking with deep emotion, 'when you gave me only part of yourself? You kept so much back, Adam. We made love, we laughed, worked together and lived as partners. But never once did you tell me you loved me. There's always been this barrier between us, this insistence of yours that you won't share whatever's eating you up because you don't want to get hurt. Well, I'll tell you something! If you love someone you have to take that risk! Oh, sure you can get badly hurt, as I am now, but there is no relationship unless you do!'

He dragged in a strangled breath, a searing agony tearing open his heart. She looked vulnerable and forlorn, her hands planted on that no longer tiny hand-span waist, her beautiful head held high in angry defiance. Her eyes swam with tears, and he could see that they were all but choking her and she was fighting for words, forcing them from her trembling lips.

'I love you,' she said brokenly. 'I always have and I always will. But I'm too proud to take you at any price and I know that we have to commit to each other totally, trust one another completely—or remain apart. I was prepared to give you everything. I expected nothing less than everything in return.' Her body drooped as if her bones had been broken. 'Oh, God, Adam!' she sobbed suddenly. 'You won't let me into your soul and you're breaking my heart!'

In two strides he had reached her. Gathered her in his arms, held her grimly while she struggled and then went limp, as if defeated and too dispirited to fight him any more.

Unfamiliar moisture clouded his eyes. Impatiently he brushed it away with the back of his hand, but she had stiffened and identified that movement, because she was looking up at him in shock.

'Adam?' she whispered uncertainly. *'Adam!'*

'I—I—' He swallowed, disconcerted by the huge wash of emotion which had engulfed him when she'd spoken his name with her old tenderness. Unable to speak, he shook his head helplessly and buried his face in her thick mane of hair.

As if co-ordinated by an unseen hand, they sank to the springy thyme on the windswept headland and clung fiercely to one another. This was where he wanted to be: in her arms, close to her heart, surrendering everything.

He took a deep, tension-laden breath and launched into the unknown. 'I love you,' he said shakily, 'more than I can say. More than I've dared to believe. You're right. Everything you say is true. I thought I could keep my past locked up in a box where it wouldn't hurt me.'

The pain came then, racking him with its intensity, and he flinched. She hugged him hard, giving him strength. He must not lose her.

She said nothing, sensing his hesitation, and raised her face, then drew his head down. Their mouths meshed and all coherent thought went with that kiss, as all his emotions flowed out to her like a river, their force, their sweetness, the incredible relief coursing through him and filling his whole body with love.

'Trish…Trish, darling, my love…'

'Don't walk away from me now,' she whispered fervently. 'I need you. Our child needs you.'

'I won't,' he promised rawly. Shaking with the depth of his passion for her, the heartbreaking spikiness of her wet lashes, the all too brutally tormented look in her eyes, he kissed her softly parted mouth and drew her around to face him. 'Listen,' he said, in a harsh, anguish-racked voice.

She was still. Adorably trusting. He swallowed hard and began.

A long, shuddering breath. 'I had a brother, Sam. A twin brother.' She took his hands in hers as he battled for control of his lungs. They were closing up. He felt the familiar constrictions in his windpipe, the infuriating weakness of his own body. Her lips touched his, then his throat. And miraculously he relaxed sufficiently to speak.

'We never knew our father. Mother found us...difficult. We didn't fit in with her young, partying image.' He focused his gaze on the turbulent seas, unable to bear the distress in Trish's face. 'We found ourselves dumped one day on the doorstep of a children's home in a strange town. We were six, but I remember it as if it were yesterday. They never traced our mother and we never looked for her.'

Her grip tightened at the hardening of his tone. The thundering waves pounded at the rocks, the sound crashing in his ears. Looking down, he saw that the tears were running silently down her soft cheeks. Tears for him. He kissed them, let his mouth work up, absorbing the salty moisture and kissing her tormented blue eyes.

'Hold me,' she whispered.

Her body pressed against his, the softness of her breasts causing him to catch his breath.

'I don't think either of us ever got over that rejection,' he said huskily. 'Sam and I grew up shutting everyone out but each other. I was his strength, he was mine, and we loved and needed one another. We did everything together. I knew he would never let me down. He knew the same.'

'And then?' she prompted gently, stroking his hair. She could feel the rippling waves of tension building up in his body, and she knew she would have done anything to make this easier for him.

He was pale, his eyes brilliant with tears he was refusing to shed. Because he would think less of himself if he did. He believed that would be unmanly. But she could see what was coming and she knew that, for Adam, the past had become a tragedy which had almost destroyed him.

'We were almost sixteen—still in the home, and about to leave after our birthday,' he said raggedly. 'W-w—' He stopped, pulling his brows together in furious frustration.

Gently she put her hands on his diaphragm. 'Remember,' she said tenderly, her voice breaking with love, 'breathe, Adam. Breathe.'

'He—he had a headache. A f-fever.'

He stopped and she saw him forcing a mastery over his voice. She felt an incredible admiration for him. He was a man who loved deeply, whose inner strength was greater than most. A man her grandfather would have been proud to know.

'You're doing fine, sweetheart,' she murmured in an undertone.

'They said—the couple who ran the home—that it was flu. They gave him medication for it and sent him to bed. I was up all night with him and I knew it was something more serious. I woke the couple up and they yelled at me. I yelled back. I tried to drag the guy out of bed and he lashed out at me. When I got back to Sam, I found that he was delirious and there was a weird rash on his body.'

'Meningitis!' she whispered, appalled.

Adam's agonised face confirmed her guess. He pushed a hand through his hair, his eyes so glazed that she knew he was not seeing anything now, only the painful images of the past.

'I stole the car keys from the hall table, carried Sam down the stairs and drove to the hospital,' he said in a raw, choking voice.

'That's illegal!' Trish burst out.

Adam gave her a straight look. 'I had to save my brother. He was crying with the pain and so was I; I swear I could feel it too. God knows how I drove. Adrenaline, I suppose. I'd never driven before! When I arrived, they took one look at Sam and rushed him to Intensive Care. They couldn't prise me away. S-Sam...died before he got there, in my arms. I felt him slip away and part of me died there, with him...'

As his voice tailed away, she drew his head to her breast. She cried for him, and soon she could feel his shoulders shaking and the breaking of the barrier that had separated them both.

A long time later he became still, his breathing normal.

Her hands stroked his hair, the curve of his beautiful neck, the broad and powerful shoulders.

'I'm so sorry, my darling,' she whispered.

He raised himself, looked at her long and hard, and kissed her with a breathtaking tenderness. 'So am I,' he said quietly. 'I missed him so much, Trish! I closed up then. Even my counsellor couldn't reach me. That was Christine,' he said, surprising her. 'She told me some of her troubles, her traumatic divorce and the difficulty of being a working mother of a toddler—partly to make me open up, I think— and I felt sympathy for her. We forged a strong, supportive friendship.'

'So you married.'

'Yes, when I was eighteen. And I'm sure now that, when she saw the chemistry between you and me, she knew that you, above anyone else, would be able to teach me how to love.' He paused. 'Trish, I want us to start again.'

'You want me to put on a green polyester frock?' she asked teasingly.

To her delight, he laughed. And then sighed and kissed her with a fierce passion that had her gasping with need.

'To hell with frocks,' he muttered. 'I want fantasy. I want a bride. At the soonest opportunity. A wife. Mother of my child. Our child, Trish!' he said fervently. 'When I believed you might be pregnant, I was rocked to the core. I knew then that I was being given another chance to love, if only I dared to take it. But I had to be sure. I couldn't bear to pour all my love into you and the baby and then be turned away.'

'I've always loved you,' she said gently.

'Marry me,' he murmured. 'Give your grandmother an occasion to wear that incredible hat.'

Trish groaned. 'You've almost convinced me that I should refuse!'

His mouth possessed hers. She lay in the cradle of his arms, absorbing his kisses, adoring the feel, the scent and the power of him. His strength. The fact that he had given her the greatest gifts of all: his heart and his trust.

Her love for him hurt so much that it was driving her to clutch at him convulsively. She needed him and he needed her. With a trembling tenderness, he dropped tiny kisses on her nose and then pushed her away, his eyes dark with hunger.

'Say yes,' he ordered hoarsely.

'Yes!' she mouthed, incapable of saying the word out loud.

Ridiculously happy, they stared at one another. His hair tumbled about his forehead, as wild as hers. His eyes sparkled as hers must.

'I adore you,' he said helplessly.

'You'll have to,' she replied, her face suddenly solemn. 'Our love will be sorely tested.'

One eyebrow lifted roguishly. 'Oh? How?'

'I think I know what Gran's wedding present might be.'

He thought for a moment. 'Not...' His eyes widened in horror. 'Not the *scarf*!' he groaned.

'And you'd better wear it,' she warned. 'I won't have you hurting my gran!'

They were standing on the quay. Stephen and Lucy, Trish and Adam, little Sam and Julia. Sam was looking at his father anxiously, waiting for the answer to the question he'd just asked.

Adam checked with Stephen, then crouched down and spoke to his small son man to man. 'If you want to keep an eye on your sister and be a page at Stephen's wedding, I'm sure he'll be very pleased. He didn't ask you because he thought you might not want to dress up. You always like to wear old things—'

'But I must look after Jules, mustn't I?' Sam said, catching his sister's little hand as if she might break into little pieces if he didn't.

'Of course,' said Adam. He gave Sam a big hug and turned to his elder son. 'That's OK, then?'

'Fine by us,' Stephen said, putting an arm around his father's shoulder.

'On the boat, now,' said Trish, bending down and getting a massive kiss from Sam. 'Wave bye-bye, Julia, darling! Sam's off to school! Have a lovely day, darling! Bye!' She wiped a little tear from her eye.

Adam's arm came around her waist. 'First day's always the worst, they say,' he told her fondly.

She sniffed and Lucy laughingly handed her a handkerchief. 'He's so little!' she protested, waving madly at the little figure in his smart royal-blue top.

'He'll be as big as his father before you know it,' said Stephen with a grin. 'Shall we go back, darling,' he asked Lucy, 'and write up the invitations?'

Trish and Adam watched them walking back to the cottage where they were living. Lucy ran the guesthouse and Stephen was on a fellowship, researching the medical properties of plants. Trish smiled fondly. Her knowledge—and her grandmother's—had come in useful to him.

'We must think of something restrained for Sam to wear,' she said to Adam as they wandered along the beach. 'No velvet trousers. I don't want him looking silly.'

'Darling,' he said with a sigh, 'if your grandmother is wearing that damn hat and I'm to be lumbered with that new scarf she's knitting for the occasion, it won't be Sam who looks silly!'

Trish giggled. 'I love you,' she said, hugging him.

'Then, when it's dark, let's go for a swim and find the camomile again, and you can prove it,' he murmured.

She smiled, lifted a radiant face and drew his mouth down to hers. 'Sentimental fool!' she whispered lovingly.

EXPECTING

She's sexy, she's successful... and she's pregnant!

Relax and enjoy these new stories about spirited women and gorgeous men, whose passion results in pregnancies... sometimes unexpectedly! All the new parents-to-be will discover that the business of making babies brings with it the most special love of all....

Harlequin Presents® brings you one **EXPECTING!** book each month throughout 1999.
Look out for:

The Baby Secret by Helen Brooks
Harlequin Presents #2004, January 1999

Expectant Mistress by Sara Wood
Harlequin Presents #2010, February 1999

Dante's Twins by Catherine Spencer
Harlequin Presents #2016, March 1999

Available at your favorite retail outlet.

HARLEQUIN®
Makes any time special ™

If you enjoyed what you just read,
then we've got an offer you can't resist!

Take 2 bestselling love stories FREE!

Plus get a FREE surprise gift!

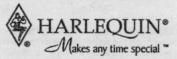

Passion

**Looking for stories that *sizzle*?
Wanting a read that has a little
extra *spice*?**

**Harlequin Presents® is thrilled
to bring you romances that
turn up the heat!**

In March 1999 look out for:

***The Marriage Surrender*
by Michelle Reid**
Harlequin Presents #2014

Every other month throughout 1999,
there'll be a **PRESENTS PASSION** book by one
of your favorite authors: Miranda Lee,
Helen Bianchin, Sara Craven and Michelle Reid!

*Pick up a **PRESENTS PASSION**—
where **seduction** is guaranteed!*

Available wherever Harlequin books are sold.

HARLEQUIN®
Makes any time special ™

Coming Next Month

HARLEQUIN PRESENTS®

THE BEST HAS JUST GOTTEN BETTER!

#2013 CONTRACT BABY Lynne Graham
(The Husband Hunters)
Becoming a surrogate mother was Polly's only option when her mother needed a life-saving operation. But the baby's father was businessman Raul Zaforteza, and he would do anything to keep his unborn child—even marry Polly....

#2014 THE MARRIAGE SURRENDER Michelle Reid
(Presents Passion)
When Joanna had no choice but to turn to her estranged husband, Sandro, for help, he agreed, but on one condition: that she return to his bed—as his wife. But what would happen when he discovered her secret?

#2015 THE BRIDE WORE SCARLET Diana Hamilton
When Daniel Faber met his stepbrother's mistress, Annie Kincaid, he decided the only way he could keep her away from his stepbrother was to kidnap her! But the plan had a fatal flaw—Daniel had realized he wanted Annie for himself!

#2016 DANTE'S TWINS Catherine Spencer
(Expecting!)
It wasn't just jealous colleagues who believed Leila was marrying for money; so did her boss, and fiancé Dante Rossi! How could Leila marry him without convincing him she was more than just the mother of his twins?

#2017 ONE WEDDING REQUIRED! Sharon Kendrick
(Wanted: One Wedding Dress)
Amber was delighted to be preparing to marry her boss, hunky Finn Fitzgerald. But after she gave an ill-advised interview to an unscrupulous journalist, it seemed there wasn't going to be a wedding at all....

#2018 MISSION TO SEDUCE Sally Wentworth
Allie was certain she didn't need bodyguard Drake Marsden for her assignment in Russia. But Drake refused to leave her day or night, and then he decided that the safest place for her was in his bed!